Boy Island

Boy Island

A Novel

Camden Joy

QUILL
WILLIAM MORROW
NEW YORK

The author wishes to thank Ben Schafer and Jonathan Moskowitz
for their support and patience.

"I Believe" by Pete Shelley © 1978 Complete Music, Ltd. (PRS), all rights
reserved, International Copyright Secured. Reprinted with permission of
Incomplete Music, Inc. (BMI). "I Believe" is from the Buzzcocks' album *A
Different Kind of Tension*.

It is the policy of William Morrow and Company, Inc., and its imprints and affiliates,
recognizing the importance of preserving what has been written, to print the books we
publish on acid-free paper, and we exert our best efforts to that end.

Library of Congress Cataloging-in-Publication Data

Joy, Camden.
    Boy island : a novel / Camden Joy.—1st ed.
        p.   cm.
    ISBN 0-688-17033-1
    1. Rock groups—United States—Fiction.   2. Rock music—United States—
Fiction.   3. Persian Gulf War, 1991—Fiction.   I. Title.

PS3560.O85 B69   2000
813'.54—dc21

99-055531

Printed in the United States of America

First Edition

1   2   3   4   5   6   7   8   9   10

BOOK DESIGN BY LOVEDOG STUDIO

www.williammorrow.com

To Somis, Spadra, and Sandusky

Boy Island

The first chapter, in which a phone call interrupts the war, a job is lost, and the little drummer boy gets swept up in the irresistible

PRESSED MUCH LATER to tell how it happened, he could recall almost nothing but a constant chill, a sense of drifting, the haunted certainty back then that even his own experiences did not belong to him. "This was at a time when I felt," he'd explain, "invisible to the naked eye."

It started with the war. He was watching it on television, smart bombs falling on CNN, when the telephone interrupted. "It's for you," his roommate covered the receiver. "I think it's that guy," meaning the one who'd called a bit earlier, claiming to be starting a band and in need of a drummer. *Not again.* Invitations of this nature arrived frequently—too frequently. Everyone apparently wanted to lead a band; nobody wanted to sit in the back, to drum. Lit with a fleeting selfishness, a few managed to assemble the pieces correctly: the songs they'd need, the musicians, the resources. For what? Some rehearsals, maybe a couple unpaying party gigs at the college. Then some member gets too cocky, someone gets bored, musicians stop speaking, band goes away.

His roommate motioned for him to take the call.

He mumbled a greeting into the phone.

"Camden Joy?"

"Yep."

His roommate snapped off the TV.

"Boy, you're a hard one to get a hold of."

No, Camden considered scoffing, not hard to get a hold of. Just blessed with a protective roommate. He draped the flannel comforter over his head, yawned, and closed his eyes. Firing through his brain came this: Televisions used to turn off differently. Funny, he'd never given it much thought. The TV image didn't blink into disappearance before the way it did now. It simply shrank until, arguably, it was gone. When he was young, Camden often stayed up late turning the TV on and off, trying to pinpoint precisely when the television was assuredly off. Over and over he hit the button and watched the on-screen image retreat to a small blue dot, which hung on for some time, as if reconsidering its departure, before slipping off into the blackness.

No, not a hard one to get a hold of; I am just a small blue dot.

Since losing his job, Camden had curled up on the sofa, like any reasonable mammal will once set on hibernating his twenties away. Occasionally a siren dashed past or an illegally over-burdened eighteen-wheeler rumbled through the intersection, steering down side streets to bypass the highway scales, creating large circles in Camden's soda. The flag above the post office would loll in the wind, craving attention with its goddamn limp waving. Camden'd set aside the rest of his days, from here on out, to be spent this way: in his apartment, dozing before the television, engine flooded, dead in the water, feelin' fine. He grew quite pleased with this picture of himself as a small blue dot. Now I'm almost there, he thought to himself contentedly. And now I'm nearly gone. . . .

Earlier that week he'd been in possession of a thing some blue-helmeted neutral observers might charitably have termed a point to his being there. Namely: a job, years spent fetching periodicals in the basement of the local library, the stacks. But he had taken too literally a posted memorandum warning against overworking, bottoming out, which could result in short tempers and gruffness. He'd gone into work at 8:00 A.M., per usual, and written his name on the sign-in sheet hanging by a metal ring on a hook beside the employee entrance. Did that, then ran into Mr. Schuck, the boss, who'd positioned himself squarely in front of the memo re: the import of adequate breaks. How long'd Camden already been there, with zero time off? En route to his locker, with Schuck right there, Camden decided to—as they say—"seize opportunity." For the very first time, he asked for a few days off.

The sound of his voice gave Schuck a start, as if he hadn't even noticed Camden. "What?" he snapped. Mr. Schuck—a pathetic, solitary figure, the forgotten principal, favored beltless polyester slacks, scuffed wing tips, wide ties. He tried looking at Camden, but in the office lighting Schuck's watery eyes slipped right past and settled on blank distance. "Oh, hello there, you," was all he came up with.

"Sorry if I scared you, Mr. Schuck."

"Nothing of the sort."

"It's just, I was thinking, well, I've been here years now, and . . . I just wondered if I had some vacation time coming anytime soon."

"What's your name again?"

Told him, Schuck harumphed, asked where Camden'd been.

"Sorry, Mr. Schuck. I don't understand."

"Where . . . have . . . you . . . been?" he asked, speaking strictly man to goat here, cruelly deliberating over each word. Rapidly asked if Camden understood this, that, and the other about library policy, didn't he realize what the libraries of northern Virginia have meant to the people of northern Virginia, didn't he *truly* value learning. Quoted Camden exact figures on—number of people holding library cards, books lent for home use in a year, &tc. Spoke of the Public Library's founding visionaries, noble public servants of yore, asthmatic Littlefield, the brilliant Miss Tessa L. Kelso, &tc.

This ran for several minutes, them standing in a poorly lit corridor, fellow employees elbowing through, nodding at the boss, winking at Camden. They pretended not to notice Mr. Schuck's flushed face, his voice rising, starting to sputter. "Schuck sucks," the employees sang at him, not-so-nicely, behind his back. "Whoa! Tough luck, old Schuck, you suck."

Mr. Schuck asked again where Camden had been.

"I've been right here." Camden's uncharacteristically exasperated. "In the library. I've been right here, in this library, doing my job."

"Strange that I haven't seen you."

A sudden chill crept up his spine when Schuck said that. It was not the first time someone'd failed to notice Camden. It had been that way at other jobs, where teenage bosses barked that he was too shy and stuck-up to handle the register, so they kept him in back tidying drawers, washing dishes, turning locks for delivery men, and stepping out of the way. Throughout everything he had been ignored, in cafeterias and locker rooms, in pep rallies and home rooms. The same guidance counselors used to introduce themselves week after week, extending a hand in welcome, saying, "You must be that new kid from our sister school to the south," saying he should come visit them when he had a moment to discuss his bright future. Teachers failed to call on him, girls failed to return timid smiles, heroic boys never acknowledged his compliments on their game-winning acrobatics or their moving oratories when addressing a classroom on the fated plight of Ophelia and Hamlet. If Mr. Schuck had said, "I haven't noticed you" or even "I haven't observed you working very hard *lately*," that'd be different. But Schuck'd asked for his name, then said he hadn't seen Camden. It made him shiver. For the thousandth time, his life became apparent as a waste. It'd been years since Mr. Schuck had seen him.

"But this is dumb, Mr. Schuck. I sign in every day, right on that sheet over there. You could just check my signature and see that I've been here every day for the last however many years."

Schuck asked if Camden thought he was a fool. Did Camden think he didn't know how many people never show up but get their friends to sign in instead?

"I don't know anything about that," Camden said truthfully.

"Well, as of today, I can assure you, a change is sweeping through our public library system."

Camden was astounded. It was true that he daydreamed, but he deserved nothing like this. Schuck dispatched him to payroll, Floor Two, where Mrs. Tilletsen's machine spat up his last check.

Whereupon Camden embraced the life of a blue dot or a

rotting log or an abandoned vehicle, albeit one that occasionally rose to use the bathroom and grab another soda. It was one of those golden eras of television, no standard programming, what with the war brewing. The story so far: A grumpy country had annexed its nice neighbor. Pillaging the neighbor's buildings of nice appliances, the grumpy troops had loaded them onto flatbed trucks to be driven back to the grumpy capital. Sanctions descended. Grumpy troops defiantly machine-gunned the happy neighbor's national zoo. They devoured the exotic animals, preparing each with a blend of mouthwatering seasonings and spiced stuffings. Camden lay captive before it, breathing shallowly. Deadlines passed unheeded. His roommate behaved as if nothing were the slightest bit wrong. But when someone called repeatedly, asking for Camden, his roommate at last handed him the phone. The person on the other end verified his name, informed Camden that he was hard to get a hold of. His roommate turned off the television. Camden covered his head with a flannel comforter. He dozed off.

"You there?"

"Yeah," Camden answered slowly. "Sort of."

"Well, hi. My name is Johnny Hickman."

"And you," Camden stretched, yawned some more, "are putting together a band."

"With David Lowery. We'll be touring soon."

"Right."

"And recording. We have a deal with Virgin."

Virgin—that was a big record company. And David Lowery, Camden sensed he should know that name. "Did you . . ." He spaced on the rest of his question, couldn't finish.

Hickman went on. "Do you know the band Camper Van Beethoven? That was David's last band. They broke up. Now me and him, we're putting together a band. You don't know any bassists, do you?"

Something dreadful happened. A clap of thunder beneath the rib cage sent blood traveling into even his furthermost limbs. To elude this unpleasant sensation, Camden threw aside the comforter and pushed himself up, thereby astonishing the soles of his numb feet with the sudden pressure of carpeting. All down his shoulders, thighs, and ankles, his bones slid wetly into place, cracking in protest. A chorus of wise inner voices beseeched him to slam down the telephone and reclaim the prone position.

It'd become apparent: This was not your typical invitation to join a nowhere-going band. Camden knew this Camper Van Beethoven, yes, had both heard them and heard of them. They were world-famous. They'd been on MTV! His roommate even possessed a few of their records. They were pop of the sarcastic kind kids Camden's age liked. David Lowery wrote their songs, played guitar, and sang. He looked kinda funny, had a big nose.

The sound, Hickman explained, would be rawer than Camper Van Beethoven. They had three weeks before the tour started. The dates were set, they only needed a rhythm section.

Camden said nothing for a great while. Inside himself a small blue dot was frantically shoving aside his inner organs, seeking room to grow. In a flash, the near dead dot had mushroomed into a phenomenally clear, wide-screen image: Lowery was singing, this Hickman beside him, while perched loftily behind them, propelling the whole affair—Camden!

Then almost at once the image transformed itself into dread, the grim fear of Christmas morning, a mute, inexplicable despair, when you admit to yourself how desperately much you want a thing but doubt you'll get it or fear it'll disappoint or agonize that the flash of joy of getting it—the rush—will rapidly fade and, anticipating this letdown, peer into the letdowns that will always await you, the dissolving satisfaction of everything.

They met the next day in a rehearsal space, two guitarists and a drummer. Hickman turned out to be a pretty fellow, dark-haired and kind. Camden tried to keep cool as his mind jumped nervously about. He'd already begun to envision the plaques the city council would distribute once native son Camden Joy became a household name. Next door to their rehearsal space, for example, was Lorusso's, which would certainly be granted landmark status, being the music store where Camden's parents got him a beginner's snare when he turned twelve. They were driving back from visiting his brother in the hospital. It was little more than a glorified bongo with plastic stars glued to its side. A consolation gift, really, because of his brother's worsening condition; nonetheless, a drum. He thought he should probably go rooting around for it in the mothballed hope chest at his mother's. It would soon belong in a memorial glass case inside city hall: the little snare he'd banged obligingly for several months before showing he could do much more.

And now here Camden was, with world-famous David Lowery and that world-famous nose of his, a nose like something pummeled from Play-Doh by two-year-olds. Lowery seemed to be following this nose as he sniffed his way toward a new, as yet unagreed upon, affront. "Music today," Lowery began, "doesn't have, like, danger anymore—or sex. I want sex—this is like, there's a few too many words in these songs. And I'm ranting. Okay?"

Camden acknowledged this to be so. Rock and roll certainly hadn't struck him as particularly dangerous of late. Rap groups seemed to be about the only bad influences anymore. Otherwise, overdoses, accidental deaths were down across the board. Grown-ups, no longer appalled, accompanied their grandkids to shows. No one covered their eyes or ears in fright. No one foresaw imminent peril or pilled themselves into oblivion like they did in the good old days.

Camden watched David sing, observing a pastiche of rage—hungry, trapped, furious, watchful, alive—reminiscent of a bird, with David's mistrustful eyes and drawn mouth and downturned beak of a world-famous nose, a frail bird, his voice barely clearing the top of his minuscule range, approaching an eruption of shrill cawing noises, his body tensed as if about to shake free his feathers and carry the drummer off in his talons.

For the most part, the songs that day began with a Hickman guitar lead over half a verse. From a drummer, these required an effect of fullness to offset the absence of words. At this point, you are conveying to the listener something akin to the sonic height of the song. You are saying, "The song gets this loud and no louder." Then, when the verse proper begins, the drums and lead guitar smoothly retreat and the vocals take their place. This fullness—lead guitarist stepping on pedals, the drummer leaning more noisily on the toms and crash—will return during the solo (which follows—or sometimes comprises—the bridge). Otherwise, the drummer stays tightly on the snare and high hat for verses (perhaps escalating with fills and off-beats), choruses usually open up with the ride cymbal taking the high hat part. The bridge might require some slightly different emphasis, a use of the toms, a double beat on the kick, a few breaks. Verse, chorus, verse, chorus, solo, verse, chorus. This is how the songs went that day. Hickman would start a song and motion for Camden to come in anytime it felt right.

Hickman and Lowery praised him highly, which had the unforeseen effect of halting the pageant of history that was scrolling through Camden's head. High praise disquieted him. Were they being sarcastic? Were they even seriously considering him? On the other hand, did he want to be considered? Although it was sometimes tough to shake free of the excruciating heaviness of his limbs, the dead jelly of legs, of cinder block hands, this was just Camden being out of shape; these were certainly not difficult songs. Any half-experienced drummer could read them quickly and supply what they required. Why did it need to be him?

Afterward, they bundled themselves up, stepped outside. Lowery leaned against a bike rack, smoking a cigarette. Hickman folded his arms and took a place on the sidewalk beside him.

Lorusso's imposed itself majestically onto the background.

It was apparent, in the way they arrayed themselves, that they desired Camden but they seemed unable, for some reason, to express this. They would not ask outright if he'd please join them. Instead, Lowery revealed how the group had no name: "For now, we're the David Lowery Band. I've had to resign myself to using my name, in order to get these bookings." His tone implied a great deal. "But it's a band, not a solo project." He encouraged Camden to suggest arrangements, covers. "It's a collaboration."

Lowery seemed effusive, avuncular. "We asked Virgin for an

advance," he smirked, "so we could go into the studio and record *a few songs* for them to hear. Just so they could decide whether to sign us. They gave us five thousand dollars. It was *so much money*, man! So instead we bought our own studio equipment, hauled it all home, set it up, and recorded this tape."

On cue, Hickman pulled a cassette from among the deteriorated stuffing of his heavy wool coat. Twenty-two song titles were listed. "Music from Big Daddy Yellow" was written on the tape's label, as well as "This is Cracker Soul." As he passed the tape to Camden, a bracing wind blew through. The trees groaned heavily. Camden's mouth felt dry. His chest tightened. Could he be getting this wrong? A small cloud momentarily blocked the sun. Camden grew afraid that if he asked for confirmation they would laugh and tell him he'd misunderstood. They'd cruelly pinch his arm, and he'd awaken as a blue dot shrinking beneath a comforter on the sofa.

Camden said he'd give the tape a listen and call them.

"You're probably wondering why Camper broke up," Lowery announced. In truth, nothing could have been further from Camden's mind. He was too busy watching Lorusso's. It had taken on a soft-focus glow, an aura of hovering magic, the tangy mystery of a fortune-teller.

As a boy, Camden passed the store daily on his bicycle, his eye caught by the shiny instruments hanging in the window: guitars, dobros, banjos, mandolins. They sold music books written in top-secret code and displayed cases of unimaginably strange items—a foreign world. He could see that one whole wall was covered with strings and cords in bright packages. Enraptured, he'd gaze in at the drum kit, the clean white skins stretched taut, the cymbals glinting in the sunlight. A pair of drumsticks had been left atop the tom as if forgotten, as if someone would momentarily return to fetch them. Straddling his bicycle out on the sidewalk, Camden'd extend his fingers, yearning to pick the sticks up. He watched kids being outfitted for the school band, equipped with woodwinds and brass. Other kids yanked harmonicas from their pockets at recess. One kid could no longer come skateboarding with him after school because of piano lessons; he had to practice for something called a recital. There was some clandestine initiation going on about which he'd not been informed. Camden dreamed of leading the school band in marches; on Christmas he'd shine during "The Little Drummer Boy." One evening his father barked at him to stop the drum-drum-drumming on everything and swore he'd show him a drumming if this continued.

"Well," Lowery summarized, getting up to go, "all I can say is, it's a long story."

Camden nodded. That evening he listened to the tape with his roommate. The songs they'd rehearsed that day still lacked complexity. Camden was crestfallen. This was not his sort of music. Jemiah Shaw—now there was someone who'd like this stuff. And so would Brenny Shaw, Jemiah's little brother. Camden went to elementary school with the Shaw boys. They wore the same clothes every day, unkempt things patched with emblems of the Confederacy. Their teeth were the color of Virginia soil. When they spoke, it was to assert that somebody they disliked was related to a black or a Jew or a homosexual. They drank beer and seemed not to have parents. They played the radio very loud, late-sixties rock music, drunken blues, seventh chords, rednecks who slept in cars, shit kickers who wouldn't apologize.

Most of the songs on this Lowery/Hickman cassette felt that

way to Camden, more like sorry country-western parodies, jokes anybody could get. A few compelled—particularly a weary ballad in which the resigned singer abandons his love to Hollywood Cemetery. The grief there felt authentic, as if Lowery too may've lost a relative.

Camden dialed David Lowery's phone number, inclined toward disinterest but unable to articulate his exact problems with this style of music. Probably Lowery wouldn't care much about the Shaw boys, even if Camden related the whole tale. Or he might decide that the Shaw boys had better taste than Camden did and prefer contacting one of them to join his band. Would that be wrong? Camden let slip that he thought the tape was "interesting," a phrase that gathered emphasis as it traveled down the phone wire. Lowery responded enthusiastically. He filled in Camden on the tour that awaited them. They'd now be winging to L.A. to audition bassists. The tour would start on the West Coast and return to Richmond in forty days.

Camden let his attention wander. The television was detailing how last night's bombing raid on Baghdad was the biggest demonstration of air power ever in military history. The next thing Camden knew, he was seated on an airplane. The takeoff was a punch in the stomach. Cities grew suddenly small. Clouds retreated to the edge of the horizon. Long blank passages of earth passed beneath. Turbulence shuddered the craft. Seat trays were in an upright locked position. Carry-on luggage was stored below the seat in front. A movie was shown about something, starring someone. A meal of cheese and chicken was served.

They landed a short time later in the inexplicably bright smear that was California.

*The second chapter, in which worries
mount, skunks and war are debated,
hearing lost, celebrities viewed, strings
broken, and gradually a band comes
together, captivating and angry*

PETE SOSDRING, BASSIST extraordinaire, had a daughter.
She was eight. She wanted a skunk. You could get them in the
mail, she said. She brought the magazine over to him one morning. The advertisement told how the stink glands were removed,
making this furry, cuddly, and easy-to-house-train mammal an
ideal house pet. It was in a magazine called *Look*. On its cover
was Judy Garland as a girl. It was from 1939.

"The company doesn't have skunks anymore."

"Where'd they go?"

"They're all dead. They're hanging from a coat hanger in somebody's closet. Oh, my little idiot. Don't look so sad. It's a real old
magazine. Remember I was telling you *The Flintstones* took place
a long time ago?"

"I want a skunk!"

"Sorry. Nobody sells skunks anymore." It felt good to sound
so certain. He closed the magazine and handed it back. "That's
why people lock their doors at night, to keep skunks from getting

inside. Nobody wants them—and Christ, how they hate us! They sit out there on the driveway every night. They want in. They'll stop at nothing. This advertisement was one of their attempts to gain entry to the home, believe it or not. I bet it was foiled just in time by Dick Tracy. Remember that movie we watched with Uncle Joseph's friend Madonna in it?" Pete's brother Joe had done a session with Madonna.

"Skunks are cute."

"No, little idiot. Mommy's cute. Skunks eat children."

"No!"

"They eat children's faces off. They have fangs as big as my fingers."

His daughter covered her ears and screamed. "I'm not listening!"

That afternoon, per union requirements, Pete went in for his annual physical. He took the hearing test, an audiogram, as he had many times before. He put on snug, cushioned earphones, signaled when he heard certain beeps and chirps, and repeated a number of words. The test concluded he had sensorineural hearing loss, that by being exposed to loud and continuous noise he was losing access to the uppermost frequencies. The physician stressed these were insignificant tones, in the area of 8,000 Hz, out of most everybody's reach. Pete disagreed; he saw his profession take a direct hit. These frequencies and a no-bullshit attitude served as his sole edge in the competitive market of sessionmen.

Driving home, there arose a howl outside the car. Cocking an ear, Pete could not be certain whether it came from animal or ambulance. He punched the steering wheel with a fist. This was beyond exasperating. It was wrong. I am losing my ear, he wanted to holler at drivers he passed. He shortened it to "fuck you," tried screaming it at the windshield several times, saw a gasoline rig and considered pointing his car straight at it—a great whoosh of flame and black smoke and that'd be bye-bye.

They went that night to watch the famous people. It was his daughter's idea, attending the Hollywood Celebrities Christmas Parade. That name got his wife's goat. She complained the whole half-hour drive there. As if they needed to put that extra word "celebrity" in there. Who else but Hollywood celebrities? What, were they gonna host a Hollywood Nobodies Christmas Parade? Or a Fresno Celebrities Christmas Parade?

Yes, Pete thoroughly adored his wife. She was still the brown-haired honey, she still had it, wasn't afraid to share it. Mostly, though, he hated how they'd turned out as a married couple, with their burdensome 2 bdr, 1.5 bths, furn, d/d, EIK, a/c, lrg closets, D/W, W/D, ww, lvg rm, yd & grge in the L.A. environs, and all the time he had to spend working to pay for it (not to mention everything it housed), how desperately he tried to appear normal, exceedingly normal, so that the neighbor kids wouldn't be mean to his daughter. ("Your dad does drugs!" he imagined them dying to shout.) Then there were just the plain adult worries everyone went through, like how he and his wife had wasted almost the entire previous night searching for a pile of warranties that they kept on file. This was not something he had ever imagined he'd be doing. Warranties, insurance forms, paper trails, bills, this was his life now, not the mad lusts and adventures he'd envisioned at eighteen. His wife of course sympathized when he bitched thus, which helped, plus he still had his bass playing, fuck yeah, though how that career would pan out now that his ear was tweaked was anybody's guess.

They got within two miles of the parade site, parked on some guy's lawn for ten bucks, and walked. The crowd of people marching with them to view the celebrities took over the streets. In every direction traffic became impossible, a mess. Cars were being locked up and left. Enterprising Mexicans took advantage by tossing booths together in the middle of the boulevards, selling illegally pirated materials, faked souvenirs of the forthcoming event, or sacks of oranges or peanuts, some even reselling Carl's Jr. hamburgers they'd just bought a short distance away. Soon the smell of these resold burgers, called (naturally) Famous Stars, was everywhere. Everyone was eating one. His daughter wanted one, then his wife, and then Pete himself. Who could resist a Famous Star? They were like a colony of ants, the advancing horde, marching and munching; or a hamburger parade, eating and tossing the wrappers, eating and tossing the wrappers. Fun, thought Pete. The scene got weirder. People slowed. Walking became treacherous, all the trash underfoot, soles greased by fast food, more and more wrappers. Now they were wading ankle-deep in garbage, each step greeted with a rotten slurp, and they were leaning on aluminum folding chairs and baby strollers to keep from falling. Pete's wife remarked that next time they'd have to work out the feeding of the mob a bit better. At some point his daughter tripped, went down, disappeared. Pete and his wife, almost laughing, dug through the garbage, as if in taking this long to come up for air the little idiot might be drowning or had gotten herself carried off by rodents experimenting with intermammalian breeding to produce tomorrow's master race. He'd watched a video about this, Pete was pretty sure, although he was terrible with movie titles. It had something to do with the apocalypse.

Momentum carried people along, a momentum soon spent. The spirit of the crowd began to droop. After all, they were kicking through rubbish to ogle celebrities. Could anybody even judge their distance to the parade site? They were close—there was the Capitol Records building off to his right. His wife thought they might even already be there. She identified the stiffening of the crowd; that was often a good sign. And she was correct, as usual, for next there came the majestic celebrities seated atop the backseats of antique convertibles, waving bravely. They were being driven right through the crowd (or so it seemed), tires crunching through a sea of burger wrappers. It was arguable who was in whose way. The people drew aside as best they could. Each car managed to squirt through. Pete plucked up his daughter, wiped her down with napkins, placed her on his shoulders. She gratifyingly commenced oohing and aahing, identifying each celebrity. *"Doogie Howser, M.D.! A Different World!* The cast of *Family Matters! Murphy Brown!* Jake MacLaine from *The Bold and the Beautiful!"*

Pete wasn't familiar with any of these shows. Back when he and his wife were first getting it on, network stars competed in track-and-field events, appearing together in fake decathlons, united as if to promote the very medium of TV. It had been a horrid thing to watch famous actors perspire in shorts and jerseys on a playing field, a mistake. They spoke of this often, Pete and his wife, and agreed that a Christmas parade was a much better idea indeed. It certainly thrilled his daughter. She was ecstatic without even realizing, of course, that nowhere else on the planet would a child's average hometown parade consist of television stars. For, growing up on the outskirts of Hollywood, Pete knew the little idiot lacked perspective, probably figured that every town on earth must have its own networks, had no way of grasping that the whole globe basically watched what she watched, and that worldwide there were fewer important networks than there were fingers on a hand.

Pete inspected the stars cruising past. They were almost within reach. People shook yuletide bells at them, asked them for money, hollered about the continuity problems of certain episodes, chucked peanut shells. The male celebrities were buff, wore patriotic suits, hair gel, they shone. The females were voluptuous, had sashes that advocated support for the gulf troops. They all looked thoroughly coked-up. Mostly Pete wanted to murder the males—in a real clumsy but deliberate manner—and fuck the females. After Santa rolled past to conclude the parade, Pete's daughter climbed down from his shoulders. She pointed out one of the gold stars in the sidewalk visible through the burger wrappers. It read "Claude Thornhill." It had the symbol for music in its center. His daughter wanted to know who this was, but neither Pete nor his wife could remember.

In bed that night he lay alongside his sleeping wife and listened to the thermostat, the clock, the fridge. Distantly, tires squealed. Then again the thermostat, the clock, the fridge; the clickings, ticktocks, and hums—these household sounds he had no trouble hearing, these ingratiating sounds of safety, of danger held at bay.

The front door of the house suddenly opened—the wrong sound at this hour!—the clunky unlatching of the lock. He sprang up. His wife stirred but slept on. He threw aside the covers and bounded down the carpeted stairs, not bothering with pajamas. The door was wide open. Fuck! If they'd only contributed to the neighborhood fund for a security patrol, if they'd chipped in on the silent alarm, the cops would already be on the way. Too late, it's always too late when you find these things out. He looked around for a weapon, grabbed an umbrella, tiptoed to the door, and peeked out.

His daughter was out there. For an instant he nearly vomited from it, the terror, the suspicion that thieves were in the middle of kidnapping his child. Then he heard his daughter's voice.

"Here." She did not sound frightened. She clapped once. "Here."

Pete stepped out to fetch her just as a car turned onto their street. Headlights swept the scene. Pete froze. *This looks bad.* "You know that weirdo Sosdring, lives on the corner? I swear I saw him after midnight *stark naked* on the front lawn with his daughter. Oh, and he was holding an umbrella, go figure." Wouldn't be but a matter of days before the neighbor kids were making fun of his daughter.

"What are you doing?" he demanded.

"Nothing."

"You should be in bed." He took her by the shoulders, steered her inside, and marched her to her room. She said nothing, did not resist.

He tucked her in and was bending to kiss her when it hit him. Duh, of course. "You were calling the skunks."

She nodded. She expected a scolding, didn't like being reprimanded.

"Ah, little idiot. I didn't mean they were out there *every* night."

"But you said . . ."

"I never said they're out there *every* night. I said they sit on the driveway *some* nights. I may've said *many* nights. But I didn't say *every* night."

"Oh."

"Okay?"

"Okay."

"But we don't want you to go looking for them. It isn't safe. Ask Mommy or Daddy. We'll set our alarm and then get up and see if there are any out there. All right?"

She said nothing. Her eyes were shut.

Back in bed, he grew scared. How could she even be awake at this hour? Pete pondered how unfair it was—when young, we have such energy but no smarts, whereas later in life, the situation is reversed (smarts, no energy). *Ain't life a bitch.* His head hurt. Everything was getting to him. Something popped in his brain, a bubble of hot lava. He could not recall how many days until Christmas. What was the point? Really, what did it matter what day today was. They were all the same. Holidays sucked, birds were dull, art was bad, nothing mattered, &tc., down a trail of depressed, quaalude-colored thoughts, at the end of which Pete stumbled upon the decision to telephone his agent. He'd find a rock band who needed a full-time bassist. Pete's life now fairly depended on it. Fuck the sensorineural hearing loss, whatever the fuck that was. He had to get back into the loud stuff.

And with that his thoughts turned wistful, concocting visions of the dream band that would save him. In the laser-lit, fog-machined concert hall of his head he heard the instruments and voices of those folks on record jackets in the seventies who stared unhappily from outdoor settings in collared shirts, intoxicated eyes squinting against the sun, their big heads gone mad with unruly, fernlike hair, ears hardly visible behind overgrown beards and sideburns, looking every awkward bit like bespectacled apes but for their platform shoes and elaborately beaded bracelets, medallion necklaces, large gold-rimmed sunglasses tinted shades of burgundy and brown, overadorned square leather hats, their expressions saying things like, "Alas, mine heart feels none of this" or "Leave me! For now I must nap" or "I dare thee to resist mine boyishness." These LP covers convinced you civilization was at the mercy of sunken-cheeked, cigarette-cradling guys who insisted upon wearing too many clothes—very high-cut, tight-crotched, floor-length bell-bottom flares; several layers of polyester blouses with astrological patterns; piles of tasseled vests; a couple leather jackets, &tc. These were the first sorts of music Sosdring had wanted to perform, stuff that once upon a time seemed like racket but lately—when these songs came pouring from a construction site or a passing car—didn't sound like racket at all. They sounded pretty groovy. He would instruct his agent to find him a band of this sort, a young band with a pulse, on the rise.

Pete's agent's office was quite close to Pete's house, but it'd been years since they had bothered to see each other. If they needed to talk, they had the telephone. For everything else there was the fax or other means. When Pete received the Lowery/Hickman demo, for example, it came by Federal Express. That was a new one. Pete put the tape on, grumbling the whole while. His agent, four miles away, rushing him parcels through some distant hub city via FedEx. What was the word, extravagant? No doubt Pete'd be the one paying for that service, he'd find the charge, printed tiny in some correspondence, among a list of absurd reimbursable expenses.

Then the music started and Pete's concerns dissolved. And even before the first song had finished, Pete knew—that's it, no turning back now. It hit him like a wave of bricks. This is the band, his gut immediately told him—I should have done this when I was eighteen.

WHEN at last he arrived in Los Angeles, a month after Christmas, Lowery asked what Sosdring thought. "There's a lot of bad vibes on this record, man," came Pete's answer, with a grave look of approval. Lowery smiled.

"Pete," Lowery later assured Hickman, "is plugged into the world in the right way."

Johnny agreed. "Pete's like one of those guys, he's an artist and he knows it, but he hates it in himself."

"Yeah, exactly," went David.

"Pete," said Hickman with finality, "is kind of a black man."

Within a short time, Sosdring was marching at the front of the band as they entered a country-western bar in southern California, a place called the Palomino, hauling equipment. They wore black Levi's, T-shirts, and various sorts of industrial shoes: heavy-soled, steel-toed Doc Martens, Skechers, that sort of item, maybe a pair of athletic shoes thrown in, black high-top Adidas or perhaps Converse. Sosdring, carrying a bass case, had natty, matted hair topping a short, pudgy body, round, half-lidded eyes, a permanently curled upper lip. Lowery was cadaverously thin with a death row stare, short strawberry blond hair, and sharp, even craggy, features. A shy Southerner called Camden Joy hauled drums, waddling a bit as he did so; narrow, trembling lips, greasy-headed, little pale eyes withdrawn behind oversize, horn-rimmed glasses. A collegiate look. Johnny Hickman came last; bushy hair in a ponytail like a big black knot of yarn, the perfect teeth and long-lashed eyes of a male model.

Someone shouted to ask if Lowery'd seen the latest *LA Weekly*, then brought one over from a stack near the door. Its cover talked about the war, something about the misery of the Iraqi civilians, who were living beneath rumors of peace proposals in the shadow of American might, skies thundering with Wild Weasels, Aardvarks, Stealth fighters, radios flowing with half-truths, hills aswarm with probes, feints, forays, unexplained skirmishes.

As the other band members returned to hauling, setting up equipment, &tc., Sosdring watched Lowery order a Miller—ah! the golden draft syrup of clear-bottled Miller, who can refuse it?—and take a seat near the rotating fan next to the cash register. Lowery read the *LA Weekly* against the bar counter, snorted, look stunned, started to call across to other band members, went back to reading, stomped his feet, banged his fist on the counter; then he took his *LA Weekly* and hurled it across the bar. It caught the current of the rotating fan and blossomed into a paper explosion. "So fucked," David muttered, passing Sosdring on his way backstage. "Just *way* fucked."

Pete retrieved the *LA Weekly*, found the page Lowery'd been reading. A picture of Lowery, pouting most alluringly. Above that, LA WEEKLY PICK OF THE WEEK. Below read:

David Lowery at the Palomino—The former vocalist of Santa Cruz's Camper Van Beethoven makes his solo Southland debut. This is the voice that launched the nouveau-hippie movement with a thousand snot-nosed jokes. Hopefully, our Davey boy has regained his sense of humor and he'll yank the boring cover of "Pictures of Matchstick Men" from his repertoire. Still longing for the halcyon days of college radio past? Trip out to here—it might be your best bet to see The Man Who Would Be Jerry Garcia. Just kidding, Dave.

Thinking retaliation, Sosdring took note of the journalist's name, then immediately forgot it—and why not? Those who can make music, do it; those who can't, write about it. Nothing they write matters.

Backstage, Pete's wife sat on a cushion with a diet soft drink, happily predicting America's defeat. Our high-tech weapons will fill with sand and break. Saddam will hurl chemical weapons at Israel, who will retaliate with nuclear weapons; then the Arab alliance will shatter. We will be mired in a Vietnam-style quagmire with the price of oil passing $60 a barrel.

Sosdring liked her idea a lot. War toughens up a generation. Good music often resulted. You need a war every so often in order to get everybody to stop bitching about meaningless shit. Privately, he was hoping that a protracted war might weed out some of those Hollywood parade twerps, leaving behind a great many curvaceous women in need of an escort.

Hickman was conversing with a guitarist he'd always greatly admired while Camden studied the mounted photos of old-time stars who had played the Palomino down through the years: silver-haired men wearing suits and string ties, some posed with stand-up basses and hollow-bodied guitars, or pictured raising an old-fashioned ruckus on the piano.

As for Lowery, he wasn't paying attention. He could think of nothing but that alternative weekly's snide recommendation, how like an obituary it read. "I would like," he told Sosdring, "for one person please, just one person, to write about music as it really is to play it, the true stuff."

Pete answered him with a look like, Must you make me *puke?* then shrugged.

Lowery understood. "I suppose nobody would read that."

Sosdring nodded.

Lowery elaborated. "They like the big, dramatic stories."

Again Sosdring merely nodded.

"Heroes. Hooks."

"Right, right."

Sosdring thought for a time how he, as a journalist—*God forbid!*—would describe the importance of this band's sound. He was used to the idea that singer/songwriters eventually tire of the noise and dissolve their rock bands to strum wimpy confessional music. This seemed thankfully far from Lowery's intent. But how to tell of this without sounding ridiculous, stirred but speechless? *One fuckin' bad-vibes cracker*—some damn turbine, charging a room with possibility.

He couldn't explain what made one want to hang around and watch anger all the time, or why being angry made one so captivating, but standing besotted beside Lowery onstage at the Palomino—an orangey evening haze clouding the doorway, his wife dressed lusciously—Sosdring sure liked what he heard. Anger.

Lowery held a trash bag in each hand. He stepped to the main microphone, yanked a wrinkled white T-shirt from one of the trash bags. "Just make me an offer," he told the audience. He displayed the shirt. It said CAMPER VAN BEETHOVEN. "I got stuck with thousands and thousands of these. Now, everything must go." He carelessly stuffed the shirt back into a trash bag. Something about the act audibly crushed the audience's spirits. The room fell silent.

"Remembrance of Things Trashed," someone muttered close by.

"Like John Lennon's *Playboy* interview," another voice muttered.

"And also," David Lowery went on, wagging a finger at the audience, "if there's anyone here tonight from the *LA Weekly*, can I just ask that you, whoever you are, just please don't write about me anymore. Please. That's just my request. Thanks."

No one spoke.

"Okay. Well." He looked up, suddenly sheepish, a three-year-old caught holding a hammer. "I'm gonna have to apologize in advance to my parents for this song. It's a prowar song." Twisting backward toward the drummer while still facing the audience, Lowery yelled "One, two, three, four!" His hand blurred into his instrument a few times. He let loose with a common little congested scream. The music was a mush of tension and rhythm.

Sosdring—his eyes clouded, lids at half-mast, features taking on much of the droopiness of the character Sarge in the comic strip *Beetle Bailey*—sought out his wife but instead only witnessed some hippie-dippie roly-poly dressed for a Grateful Dead show wriggling at the front of the stage—Look at Shamu flopping there, Sosdring thought—all these barefoot, pot-and-patchouli Camper fans are like fucking Orcas.

Sosdring swung into exaggerated, marionettelike vitality, bobbing his head, face animated, wrenching open his eyes, lifting his brow scornfully. A visible shiver went through the crowd. People near the center began to shove one another in time to the music. A few spectators attempted to take notes. Holding pens and notepads, they raised their arms as if in surrender, trying to stay above the fray and stand where it was calm. *Fucking journalists.* Pete glared as they scribbled madly above their heads. What a ridiculous spectacle. *This song is lost on you people.* The audience continued pushing one another and, wonderfully, a journalist got his granny glasses knocked off. Kids roared. Sosdring lost his place in the song. Eventually, somehow, it came to a glorious end. Lowery took off his red guitar. He set it on the side of the stage, walked behind the drums, strapped on an identical-looking white one, and then counted off another great song.

The band's manager, a broad-faced, casually dressed man of medium height, materialized amid all the squall and bellow. He was studying the red guitar as a doctor might a patient, one hand settled on the guitar's body, the other laid gently on the neck. He appeared to be counting the strings. He reached down, snapped open a small tool kit at his feet, took out a square paper envelope that said ".13," removed a nimbly rolled silver guitar string, and shook the string into full length.

Pete's wife stood beside the manager. They had met backstage and had some fun together ridiculing Marilyn Quayle. The manager set the tool kit to the side, where Pete's wife saw empty drum cases, guitar cases smothered in bumper stickers. Those that went with David Lowery's instruments were covered in airline transport stickers, electrical tape; stenciled on the cases in white paint was "CVB."

Pete's wife linked it all up: the abbreviation CVB derived from the words Camper Van Beethoven; the lyrics that warned them of Lowery's burden, derived from those trash bags full of T-shirts he was stuck with; his anger at the *LA Weekly*, derived from the tone of a condescendingly chummy review.

The manager finished restringing the guitar and leaned it up in a guitar stand in the middle of the stage. "Not really my job." The manager cupped his hands, screaming into her ear to make himself heard. "If David wasn't such a cheapskate this band would get a roadie. . . . I have a feeling they'll need one."

She grinned.

Two songs later, Lowery broke another string.

➺ *The third chapter, in which the band sets out, rock and roll injuries are detailed, the tonnage game explained, cigarettes smoked, juvenile delinquents met, and a radio interview heard in a hotel*

THEY HEADED EAST, four musicians in a family vehicle—a rented minivan—stopping once a day to play before people, then driving on. American flags flew from porch stoops and car antennas; overpasses were slathered with anti-Arab sentiments.

They tried on various roles in the minivan. Someone would be reading a book—some tale of mayhem or a Richard Brautigan–style comedy—telling everyone else to pipe down; reading one page, slowly lowering the book, drifting away, looking groggily out the window, commenting absently. Someone else would not speak except to talk about being hungry or needing to use the bathroom. Someone tried to nap, head back, mouth open, eyes shut, periodically muttering flat replies to the teasing comments quietly being directed at him. The remaining musician drove the vehicle while broadcasting nonstop about the other drivers on the road, the filth on the windshield, the mysterious source of a cold air leak only he could feel, distractedly reading aloud passing billboards, talking about the music on the boom box. The sights and sounds of nature did not count. They traveled some concrete corridor solely candied with cheap commercials, intent on ignoring all that was mute and colorless, and were thus not seeing how the Mojave pines gave way to Arizona shrub, how the hills drew near then receded, how the gray, dusty sparrows of the desert became the bluish blackbirds of the Southwest, their call deepening handsomely. A shooting star meant less than a lit cigarette tossed from a speeding car. The only real things to these four were made by men in the last few years, and nothing else existed.

They could not elude the war, the live audio feeds from journalists in Iraq's capital who heard roosters crow, bombs fall, antiaircraft pops. Defense Secretary Richard Cheney busily told reporters nothing. There were reports of peasants fleeing into Jordan, diplomats being expelled, planes striking at the elite Republican Guard in northwest Kuwait with armor-piercing cluster bombs. Muslims demonstrated around the globe in support of striking Israel—"Allah willing, this will be the end of Israel, for it should not exist and it must not exist"—while in sealed rooms across Tel Aviv, children vomited in gas masks as parents pulled syringefuls of the anti–nerve gas serum atropine.

Looking for a change of subject, David astonished them with a description of Bedrock City, AZ, a nearby community that consisted of a massive, life-size replica of the characters, dwellings, and vehicles featured in Hanna-Barbara's *Flintstones* cartoon. Afterward, they stopped for gas, piled out of the minivan to partake of cigarettes—they had all taken up smoking hand-rolled cigarettes—and, looking up, found themselves at the fort from the

TV show *F-Troop.* Someone screamed, expressing the concern for all of them that from here on east, the highway would be lined with discarded TV shows. First Bedrock City, then the *F-Troop* fort; next they'd pass the KAOS headquarters from *Get Smart,* then the nightclub from *I Love Lucy,* the ranch from *Bonanza,* the exteriors from *All in the Family.*

They might never leave Hollywood.

This fort, this once familiar sight on the boob tube, was now a combination gift center/gas station/bus stop/diner. Hickman went in to pay for the gas, found several people asleep before quiet rental TVs, their heads slung sideways over the arms of their chairs, dreaming of more television landscapes. Others, arguably awake, watched Johnny with tranquilized eyes; to them, with his perfect good looks, Johnny looked like he'd been peeled straight off a TV screen. While the cashier did her math, he poked listlessly through Desert Storm key chains, patriotic license plate holders, and souvenir *F-Troop* postcards held in a wire stand in the corner. Pictures of Sergeant Agarn, Larry Storch, Ken Berry. Behind the postcard stand, several faxes were Scotch-taped to the wall. One showed a camel with a SCUD missile lodged in its mouth. The camel's testicles were on a wood block, over which a Bedouin stood with his sledgehammer raised high. The caption read: IRAQI MISSILE LAUNCHER. Another was a fake letter to Saddam from our president on official stationery, which began "I'm sure after I explain my feelings on the matter you will undoubtedly see my point . . ." and degenerated into "Read my lips! Get the fuck out of Kuwait you raghead son-of-a-camel-humpin' bitch . . ."

Johnny took the change from the cashier and left, feeling no urge to speak to the others of what he had seen.

On the radio came the latest stats—30,000 sorties, 8,500 tank kills, 533 EPWs, 600 armored vehicles destroyed, 1 Raven (ours) shot down—followed by an old Pointer Sisters' song. "We will never escape the shitty music of the past," someone in the mini-van declared fervently, "no matter how fast we drive." It was supposed to be funny.

"Fuck you, shitty music!" Pete defended the song. "Who calls this shitty music? I played on this cut!"

A bruised silence hung low in response, for it was not a question of shitty music at all, but rather how trampled one finds the past, and where this urge to conquer things comes from; and naturally there was no way to talk that out.

"We have to cover some Camper songs," Lowery announced.

"Not," answered Sosdring. "Camper. Is. Dead. Get over it. Shock Orca."

"It's fair for them to expect some."

Camden stirred. "That song you wrote, that Camper song."

"Yeah?"

"The one about Jack Ruby."

"Yeah," said Lowery. " 'Jack Ruby.' That's its title."

"Uh-huh."

"So? What about it?"

"Oh. . . . My roommate played it once for a girlfriend."

"Yeah."

"About halfway through, she goes, 'Where did Jack Ruby go?' "

"Really?"

"Yeah, and so my roommate, he goes, 'Oh, he's still in there, buried somewhere in there.'"

"That's good, yeah. Man. That was Virgin's fault, they made me shorten 'Jack Ruby,' it used to be about fourteen verses long. They fucking hated that whole album, they just thought it was too trippy, man, couldn't be marketed."

There came and went a lukewarm winter rain—noticed by the band only through the pinging of ridiculous polyrhythms on the minivan's roof—a tender drenching that smelled of sprouted seedlings and chimney smoke. Cows stood bewildered in wet pastures, calling in their strange tongue for there to be an end to the world, while football games in schoolyards continued apace, muddy and exhilarating. A laser-guided bomb strayed from its path, hit a crowded marketplace in the city of Fallujah, and killed 150 civilians.

FAR down the length of Dallas's Elm Street, seventeen blocks from the Greyhound station, past closed malls, parking structures, gun shops, and video arcades, after heading under a freeway and passing out again, there began a neighborhood called Deep Ellum (as in, deep into Elm Street). Deep Ellum was a bohemian neighborhood of galleries and artists' spaces, neon facades, a well-groomed clientele of comfortably dressed art patrons lingering about.

Deep into Deepest Ellum could be found the Da Da Club. It had a sophisticated, upscale feel—faded brick, natural lighting, open air restaurant, tables set up right to the brink of the stage.

The bar was a place of quiet elegance where the cheapest Miller on tap cost $3.50.

The band smoked at a table in back. They had just completed their meal. David Lowery was speaking. "When Camper went to Europe on the Key Lime Tour, we each had one: 'the Five Rock and Roll Injuries,' we called them."

"Oh yeah?" said Johnny. After all their years of friendship, David still managed to surprise him with hilarious stories.

"Yeah. Like, let's see. Well, mine was, I remember I was sitting on the bus and I turned to talk to someone and I coughed. And somehow, like, I must have pulled some muscle in my sternum. It hurt to sing for a week. So that was the first rock and roll injury."

Everyone laughed.

"What were the others, let's see. Greg Lisher . . . he was walking up some stairs with a backpack over one shoulder like this, and he was trying to take a bite out of a sandwich in his other hand and somehow he tweaked his shoulder. David Immergluck was shitting on a Turkish toilet when money spilled from his pocket and he tried to catch it and strained his back."

"Were these all back injuries?" Camden wanted to know.

"No, no. In fact, the best . . . well, the best was Morgan. She was limping one day and so I asked her, I said, 'Hey Morgan, did you hurt your ankle?' She told me that, well, I guess she was masturbating in the bathtub and her orgasm was so strong, she clenched her foot—"

Pete Sosdring exhaled a long stream of tobacco smoke. "I like this Morgan chick."

"Yeah, she kicked the spigot or something when she came, and her foot wouldn't unclench."

"I see," said Camden.

"The perils," said Johnny, "of rock and roll. And now, Morgan's off with Jane's Addiction. Betcha she'll break them up, too. Just watch."

"Dangerous stuff," nodded Pete. "This rock and roll."

"And Victor's was . . ." David faltered. "What was it?"

"Some boy hugged him too tight or something," proposed Pete, always ready with the insults. "Playing with gerbils and one got stuck."

"No no. Victor's could've been blisters. I think he was walking in bare feet in Florida. But no. That might have been a previous tour, not *Key Lime*."

Camden began to sneeze.

"You getting sick?" Hickman tenderly asked.

"Better not be," warned Lowery.

"You get me sick," said Sosdring, "I'll fucking kill you."

The conversation turned to something called "tonnage." They were competing this tour not simply to sleep with the most women but to rack up the highest possible tonnage. A tonnage point was earned for each girl-pound successfully seduced. If one bedded a two-hundred-pound female, this would be equivalent to bedding both a ninety-pounder and a one-hundred-and-ten pounder, even though the latter efforts presumably required more time. Thus, as a woman's worth in this game was calculated by her weight, they were encouraged to defile the plump over the slender.

"This is so fucking twisted," chuckled David.

"You say that," went Pete, "because you're losing."

"I'm not losing, man."

"No. You're in third."

"I got Krishna the Goddess of Love in San Diego and that biker chick in Tucson."

"And they weighed?"

"Each was at least a hundred and twenty pounds."

"Right. You have two hundred and forty points. You're in third."

"Third is not losing, man."

"Put it this way. You're only beating Camden, who has zero."

"Ouch," responded Camden.

"It's okay," Johnny placed a sympathetic hand on Camden's shoulder. "It's a long tour. You'll get yours."

"Rub some meat on it," advised Pete with a sneer. "And the dog'll lick it."

"So how many points was last night?" asked David.

"Well." Pete performed some silent calculations. "This special friend was heavier than she looked."

"What, you put her on the scale?"

"I only mean, she was a whale. A hundred fifty-five pounds, easy."

"No way!"

"Way. She had one of those ripe asses—Yogi Berra coulda hid a pic-a-nic basket between those cheeks of hers."

"Pete always tries this," Camden muttered.

"We all saw your special friend," Johnny argued. "She was short. I say one-fifteen. Even one-twenty is pushing it."

"Yep," said Camden.

"Absolutely," said David.

Pete shrugged in acceptance. "But I should score extra for the trouble it took this morning."

"You should lose points for the trouble it took, man. Can't believe you, we're already out of town and on the highway when you realize you left your suitcase with this chick." David relived the story, though they had all been present to experience it the first time.

"And I never got her name."

"And you didn't know her name, her address, her number, nothing."

"But," Pete pointed out, and with his chubby fingers he made the A-OK sign. "I remembered where she worked."

Camden choked on some smoke. "Only twenty-five thousand people work there. At the university."

"So we drive back to the University of Texas," David continued. "We all split up, looking for this chick."

"Yeah, well." Pete was finished with his cigarette. "Eventually we got my suitcase back, that's all."

"She was so surprised to see you again, man," Johnny laughed.

"It was hard," said David. "We had to like con these security guys into letting us into the computer area. Remember? We said that you were about to have an asthma attack and had given this woman your inhaler by accident."

"She looked surprised," Johnny repeated.

"She was surprised, all right," said Pete. "Man, this is the tour I should have done when I was eighteen!"

"It's lucky we got to Dallas on time." David emphasized the

words with jabs of his cigarette. "You should lose tonnage points, man."

"Blow me."

"Ah! My stomach hurts." Camden pointed at David's plate. "I shoulda got what you got."

"Great," said David in a sinister voice. "Then I could've eaten *yours*."

THE band soon scattered; they had finished sound-checking before their meal, so now David went to a radio interview, Camden to a bookstore, Pete to swim laps at a nearby YMCA, and Johnny down Elm, a half mile to their hotel.

Johnny paused at a newsstand to examine various headlines—the air war went on—enemy warplanes attacked while inside reinforced concrete hangars, fire control radars devastated, their runways blasted, rutted, inoperative. Baghdad's supply officers drove several thousand head of cattle south to Iraqi troops to feed military encampments their first beef in many months; twelve POWs taken when American marines took possession of Kuwaiti offshore oil drilling rigs to launch artillery inland; combat search-and-rescue missions being conducted to find allied MIAs in the heart of Iraq.

He began again to walk and soon had struck up a conversation with a collection of big girls at a bus stop. Perhaps this testified to Hickman's devotion to the tonnage game, because these big girls appeared, on the whole, thoroughly unapproachable, breathing fury in untucked plaids, black jeans, and flat Nikes.

These were the sort with buffed maroon fingernails long as ice picks, who chewed gum with their mouths hanging open, chins bucking in and out, threat-filled girls with swaggering eyebrows, bragging all the while how their brother's gonna "kick your ass."

Among them, though, was an anomaly: a chatty girl on the bus bench gaily swinging her legs, which were too short—when she sat upright—to reach the sidewalk. The girl introduced herself to Johnny as "Michelle Bee-Kay-Hey Rat or Termite."

Johnny asked what "Bee-Kay-Hey" meant.

"It means like 'better known as,' like initials." She talked compulsively; the older girls stewed. She said she was a Crip but her boyfriend was a Blood and she was fresh from eight months at a juvie facility they call Statestown, heading home to her grandmother.

Hickman balked at someone so young being a gang member, so she showed him the signs and shakes of the Crips and Bloods and then, for good measure, the Kings and the Bros. Then she regaled him with gang codes—"Dallas is D-Town," she explained. "San Antonio is Sananton, Houston is H-Town, Brownsville is Browntown, you see, 'cause Brown you see is the first half, that's the same, and suppos'ably ville, that part is like town."

"Is," Johnny asked, "Austin a town or 'A-town'?"

She answered very seriously. "No. Austin is Austin."

He asked about her feelings on the war.

"Stupid A-rabs," she replied, "they kill all these people, then we do it and they don't like it? Taste their own medicine. Can't we 'pow' knock out that creep, what's-his-name, huh, like a snub-nosed .357?"

She wore ankle-high sneakers, a knee-length skirt, an oversize white blouse knotted in such a way as to reveal a black T-shirt underneath. Hickman glimpsed the side of her face—red, pouty lips; round, full cheeks; thick, dark, shoulder-length hair parted down the middle; saucy, coquettish eyes of brown—and slowly looked away. Thirteen, he thought dully. Thirteen years old, tops.

"So, like, who are you guys, you famous?"

"Not yet."

"Like, what do you play?"

"Rock and roll."

"New wave?"

"Okay. Okay, maybe."

"I like rap, Aerosmith, new wave, and metal."

He wanted to respond that she'd love them, wanted to invite her to tonight's show, but he held his tongue. Several thoughts collided at once—this girl was too young, he was asking for trouble, she didn't need another horny adult but decent fatherly advice. The image of his own son came to mind, and all sexual interest immediately exhausted itself. Johnny let the look on his face say that he was a concerned buddy, nothing more.

In Statestown, she piped up suddenly, they wouldn't allow anyone to have Polaroid snapshots, because they could be cut open and inhaled for the high.

"Even once they're dry?" he inquired.

"Yeah, don't you know?"

Johnny tried to tell her then about the unofficial runaway shelter he and his wife had operated back when they were teenagers. Well, not so much a runaway shelter as a place for strays to crash when they had nowhere else to go. One of the boys who would sleep on the sofa from time to time was a lanky redhead who made up funny songs on the acoustic guitar. This was how he first met David Lowery, who now led their not-yet-famous new wave band. And the moral of the story is . . . ?

Michelle wasn't hearing him. She sniffled and snapped her gum. She was looking at nothing, just the fraying back of the polyester backpack she held in her lap. What made her seem so brave, Johnny wondered. Is this love? They'd marry and of course, yes, be happy, but one day there'd come a knockin' at their door and there by golly would stand the community judges, in their fists a petition signed by all, demanding to know the meaning of this, he with a near Mexican wife less than half his age, was she daughter, lover, housekeeper, but his mob-calming answer would so madden the new wife she'd advance toward him later that same night, as if in seduction, while clutching behind her back a four-star, seven-inch serrated knife manufactured by J. A. Henckels Zwillingswerk of Solingen, Germany, and minutes later he'd be on the phone to emergency services and the community would be all I told you so.

Michelle continued—she was Level One, which meant she got three changes of clothes, no jewelry, no pictures at all, curfew at 6:00 P.M., fifteen minutes for meals, and strictly no contact with boys. But riots kept occurring in Statestown between the Crips and Bloods and then she'd get together with Leonardo (b.k.a. Kid), who would slip in and bust her out. Together they'd hide beneath the pinball machine on the fifth floor for hours.

Before any more could be said, someone came by and picked the girls up, and they vanished into the Dallas evening.

Hickman went in search of garish neon, a sex shop where he could masturbate, to avail himself of filmed scenarios in which swimsuits came off, gym clothes came off, blouses and under-garments came off, stockings came off, and escalating moans were exchanged. He found one two blocks over and afterward headed back to the hotel room.

Upon entering, the phone began to ring. Camden was there to pick it up. He said yes a few times and hung up.

"That was David on the phone just now," he told Johnny. "Calling from the radio station. He told me, whatever I do, not to eat the candy bars in the refrigerator. They cost two dollars apiece." He rolled his eyes, sighed.

"Sorry. It's, like, David sometimes . . . he pinches pennies."

"He's tight," said Camden. "Runs a tight ship."

"Yeah," said Johnny. "But it's also, that's something I love about him. He's got these qualities. Like sometimes he'll use a bottle cap as an ashtray, it's so fucking incredible, putting out his cigarette in this little thing. He's Virginian trash. He's a cracker."

"A bad-vibes cracker," Camden quoted Pete.

The phone rang again. Camden answered it without enthusiasm, listened for a moment, let out a chuckle, put the receiver down. "That was David calling back. He said—I quote—'AND OH GOD DON'T GO NEAR THE TOILET—THAT COSTS A QUARTER A FLUSH!!!' "

Camden went to take a shower and emerged afterward to find Hickman sitting on the bed, scratching out a stick figure on hotel stationery.

"What is that you're doing?" Camden asked, scrubbing his hair with a towel.

"It's for my son."

"Your son?"

"He's three."

"You know, I didn't realize you were married."

"I'm not. Pete's married. I'm separated."

"Hunh."

The television played with the sound turned off. *The Oprah Winfrey Show*. Johnny used to watch *Oprah* while jacking off. One time when he came, he accidentally bumped the channel switcher, seeing—even as the orgasm still washed over him—a leopard on an animal program, ears back, a drugged stare, blissfully postcoital, numb and pure somehow, and Johnny so immediately identified himself with that leopard that for a second they were one and the same, a johnny leopard wondering how it'd gotten into this house and whose television set this was.

"My divorce," Johnny explained, drawing a deep breath, "will be final the night we play Alexandria."

"I'm sorry," Camden said. "I don't mean to . . . you know."

"Not a big deal." By which Hickman meant to reassure himself that hearts get broken, that's just what they do. By which he meant he was trying to live with this feeling in his chest that a jar of canned tomatoes had exploded from the presence of contaminants (or quite possibly an imperfect seal) and infected the quiet in his soul with rot. "Divorce is in the air or something. You know, most of these songs we're playing, they're about David's breakup with his girlfriend. She broke up with him, after, like, five years. Right after that, Camper broke up."

"Then he called you."

"Then he called me. That's true. He sorta summoned me to Virginia."

Camden went over to the hotel radio and turned it on. "I think David's on soon." He flipped around, settled on one station. Bored teenagers quoted Reuters that guided missiles had killed 1,100 civilians in an air-raid shelter outside Baghdad this morning. This segued into noise recorded by bands Johnny didn't know.

"So what was she like?" Camden asked, voice limp as old lettuce. "This girlfriend woman of David's."

"I met her at the show in San Diego," answered Johnny. "Didn't you see her? She was . . ." A little too bony, tall black heels, two dark circles for eyes, a little hyphen of a mouth. Fingers tipped with bandages, the corners of her mouth drawn protectively around her teeth like halfbacks brought close to guard the goalie. "She had . . ." A watch on a wide leather band, a big, black heavy purse in her lap, hair pulled back with two side wisps dangling loose and falling forward to parenthesize her forehead. The lime-green squares of her dress, her black bra strap inching elbow-ward. Was that thing on her lip herpes? What made her seem so brave? Was this love? They'd marry and of course, yes, be happy, but one day there'd come a knockin' at their door and there by God would stand longtime friend David Lowery, in his fist a pistol cocked to fire, demanding to know the meaning of this, he with David's one and only honest-to-God true love, was she bound, trapped, kidnapped, but his friend-calming answer would so madden the new wife that she'd advance toward him later that same night, as if in seduction, while clutching behind her back a circular knife blade made in Japan for use in the Custom 11 Cuisinart and minutes later he'd be on the phone to 911 and David Lowery would be all I told you so.

"Was she smart?"

"Yeah," said Johnny. His eyes were dark as cola. "It was fucked."

"Five years. Jesus."

"Yeah."

San Diego, the show after the Palomino, was also where a beauty had come up to Lowery after the show—Krishna, the Goddess of Love—announcing, "I want you to fuck me." This had prompted them all to agree that this tour bespoke great tidings; since then, though, Hickman was genuinely distraught at how few chicks this band got.

He went back to his son's drawing. Camden could see where Johnny had put a big guitar around the stick person. "This is Daddy," he wrote at the bottom. He drew an arrow pointing at the guitar-laden figure.

"So that song 'St. Cajetan,' is that who that's about, his last girlfriend?"

"I don't think that one so much." He repeated the song title, laughed to himself.

"Well, who is Saint Cajetan anyways?"

"The patron saint of water. No, I really don't know. It's so funny. David, of course, the master of mispronunciation, likes it to be Saint Caj-uh-tan, but it's really pronounced Caw-he-tan; he just won't do that. It's more Virginian trash this way."

"So there is no Saint Cajetan?"

"Oh, I don't know about that. I know the title's from, Camper used to play a church-turned-club called the Saint Cajetan."

"So that one's maybe more about the Camper breakup?" Camden asked.

Johnny shrugged. "I suppose."

The music ended, and an enthusiastic young woman with a Texan drawl came on. "But we have another special guest!" she chirped. "We've had special guests in our studio all day today, and to top everything off now we've got David Lowery in the studio!"

David grunted a low syllable.

"How are ya?" she asked.

"I'm okay." This was not the David Lowery who had held court at the lunch table an hour before. A weary disappointment hung in his voice. He sounded not only older than this disc jockey but flintier, more beat-up.

"Recovering from a cold?" the interviewer went on gamely. "Or just starting on one, at least?"

"A little bit, but it's okay. I feel the normal amount of tired from touring . . . with a little bit of a stopped-up nose."

"Yeah," she cooed sympathetically.

She sounds good-looking, thought Johnny. David is always *so* lucky. Johnny put aside his son's drawing and imitated Lenin lying in state, hands folded across his chest. He studied the ceiling as he recalled a Portuguese prostitute with her prosthetics, a painted dollhead set upon a voluptuous body, something both slight and aggressive about the frame, a charged potential for the erotic—was that smile sincere? Was that thing on her lip herpes? What made her seem so brave? Is this love? They'd marry and of course, yes, be happy, but one day there'd come a knockin' at their door and there by gosh would stand her former employer John Pimp, in his fist a bottle busted open, demanding to know the meaning of this, he with John Pimp's one and only honest-to-God best whore, was she happy, healthy, horny, but his pimp-calming answer would so madden the new wife she'd advance toward him later that same night, as if in seduction, while clutching behind her back a linked length of anchor chain forged in the eighteenth century for securing schooners to the Mediterranean seabed and minutes later he'd be on the phone to the *polícia* and John Pimp would be all *eu disse-te que sim.*

"People will know you best from your work with Camper Van Beethoven."

How much you wanna bet this DJ's blond, Johnny mused. "She sounds blond, don't you think?"

"Okay," said Camden. He absently tugged his fingers, looking tiredly at the flowered wallpaper.

"Wonder how much she weighs," Hickman moaned. Big, fat, blond southern belle. We're talking tonnage. Bet her linen suit becomes transparent in a thundershower and she runs down the street like Hot Lips in *M.A.S.H.*, one hand down, one arm across.

"And now," the young woman continued, "you have been working on some solo stuff."

"Well, yeah," David spoke, distant and apparently still unable to chase down his thoughts. "Kind of working on some solo stuff. Camper broke up. I moved to the South. So I mean, I guess . . . that's what you call solo stuff."

The interviewer giggled nervously at his flat tone.

"Actually I have a band," David remembered, and suddenly his voice rose with vigor. "It's not me solo, it's a whole band. Well, there's four of us. One of the guys is from the same town that I grew up with—er . . . from the same town I grew up *in*."

Another giggle.

"In southern California. When the band broke up, I went to Morocco."

"Oh."

They always sound so disappointed, Hickman thought, that he went to Morocco. It's like they want to hear how he expatriated his lazy hide to the beach, where he lived for months bartering for homemade protein blends in exchange for guitar picks, living the undeniably good life until the savages cut the phone lines and he had to retreat upriver, keeping the sun to his back and praying vainly that the beekeepers didn't inform the G-men of his whereabouts.

"After I went to Morocco, I just decided I wanted to work with this guitarist Johnny, and so we eventually put this band together."

"Uh-hunh. Who else is in the band?"

"Um," answered David.

"Watch," Camden quietly put in. "He won't say my name."

"What are you talking about?" Johnny snorted and then smiled generously. "Of course he will."

"He never does," said Camden.

They held their breath, watching the radio like it would burst.

"There's this guy," David answered with a sigh. "Pete Sosdring. From L.A. Plays bass."

"And?" Camden asked the radio.

"And there's a drummer."

"See?" said Camden.

"Oh," went the interviewer. "And how would you describe your sound, I'd have to say it seems more, more . . . regressive."

"More what?" asked Johnny. His fantasy of fucking the disc

jockey immediately took on a decidedly darker hue. He ran his hands over the soft blue bedspread, which was thickly stitched and felt tough, like the face of a killer in a horror movie.

Camden agreed. "No, I know what she means. I keep thinking how this sounds like a band that predates David's last one."

Contemplating this, Johnny realized he had actually *been* in the precursor to David's last band.

This was back in their hometown, a classic dullsville, where culture was whatever magazine they happened to stock at the strip mall, where girls described themselves as either "um, all like" or "like um, all"—the last community one passed if, abandoning the West Coast, one fled toward the desert. Every afternoon, courtesy of the prevailing easterlies, they received L.A.'s smog secondhand. At the time, Hickman was Johnny Danger of the Dangers, a legendary local punk group, and David had grown from teen stray to bassist in the other legendary local punk group, their rival, Sitting Duck. One summer David decided to bring together "the best musicians in the Inland Empire," formed the Estonian Gauchos. The Gauchos stayed together a month—until everybody had to go back to school.

Johnny and David entertained themselves lately by trying to recall precisely what the Gauchos had played. Things rose foggily to mind. They had done smug jokes in funny voices, ska versions of "Louie, Louie" and "Tom Dooley," and reggae classics. Their sound hadn't been very punk. They'd grafted Chuck Berry licks onto mariachi music, which was David's idea, an experiment. They'd also covered Sitting Duck songs, like the lightly skipping keyboard instrumental "Skinhead Stomp," its upbeat less harsh than ska, more lilting than reggae, wrapped about a wobbly Middle Eastern espionage style melody—klezmer on Casio,

The Gauchos played one gig, a party at Lowery's parents' house. They played a set, stepped aside to permit the very loud Festive Shapes to play, and were preparing to return to play their first set all over again when the curfew clock struck ten, and the police showed up. David went up to the cops, screaming face-to-face, "Get off our property! You can't be here—this isn't Poland!" A huge cheer went up. Hickman seemed to remember that this earned more applause than their band did.

Next summer, home again from college, David started up another band: Camper Van Beethoven. David and Johnny stayed in touch through the next several years and in 1986, when Camper's guitarist, Greg Lisher, had considered quitting, David asked Johnny if he could replace Lisher. Hickman couldn't see dissolving his new band, the Unforgiven, and giving up his momentary gig as opener for Tom Petty and ZZ Top. It took the breakup of the Unforgiven and Camper Van Beethoven—just as it had earlier taken the breakup of the Dangers and Sitting Duck—for Johnny and David to again play music together.

"So you just set up a tape deck," the interviewer was saying, "in your house in Richmond and you and your guitarist sat around and did these songs?"

"Yeah. For like four months and stuff. Yeah. We wrote thirty or so songs. We wrote this record, which we haven't recorded yet, and we got a record deal. I don't know. Everything seems a little out of order or something. We're touring right now, but we haven't done a record or anything."

"So are you gonna call it . . . when it comes out, is it just gonna be David Lowery's record, or is there gonna be a band name?"

"Uh, there's gonna be a band name. I can't tell anybody what it's gonna be called yet 'cause I've had this bad luck with picking a couple names and finding out someone else has them."

"Uh-oh."

"So I'm refusing to tell anybody this name that the band's gonna be called. I could have called us anything on this tour, I could have called us—"

"Crazy Sloth!" Johnny shouted at the radio.

"Galoché Moderna!" yelled Camden.

"I could have called us 'Cup' or whatever," said David very slowly, "and nobody would have known who we were. So we decided to just tour under my name. But yeah, it's a band, it's not a solo project."

"Good. Okay. We just had a caller call up with a question for you. It goes, ummm . . . 'When you eat an orange, do you cut it in quarters or peel it?'"

"I peel it."

"Really? Wow! Okay then, do you tear each orange slice, y'know, opening the sheath, or are you careful to, like, detach each of the, uh, pouch things?"

"Hmmm. Well, I'm a pretty messy orange eater."

"Oh. Are you?"

"Yeah."

"Okay. And the other question is 'Are you a Virgo?'"

"No."

"Well, then yeah, *of course*. I mean."

"God." Lowery chuckled.

In the motel room Hickman shook his head sadly. "And parents thought *my* generation sounded dumb on the radio."

Camden issued an exhalation.

"So then," the disc jockey said. "About this next song."

"Yeah."

"Well."

"Have you already listened to it?"

"Yeah. And I guess what I want to know is, is this song directed at someone?"

"Huh?"

"When you sing about how we need another folk singer like a hole in the head, is that directed at some folk singer in particular?"

"No. Nobody in particular. If you listen to the lyrics, it's kind of about that, but it's not really. Someone's wigging out about something. And they keep *talking* about folk singers. But that's not *really* what they're wigging out about. I mean, you finally get the punch line by the third verse—'What the world needs now is a new Frank Sinatra *so I can get you in bed.*'"

Another giggle.

"That's what it's about. It's about sex. And, like, it's about diversion. It's like chickens; when one gets beaten up it beats up another one even though it's really mad about something else. You understand what I'm saying?"

"Chickens."

"No?"

"Well, let's go ahead and listen to at least this song from the cassette."

"Okay, fine."

"Something a little different," observed the interviewer, "rather than that cool, clean production studio sound."

"What?" yelled Johnny.

David politely disagreed. "Well, actually, I'm kind of proud of it. It's maybe a little bit slick, but it's still like homemade slick."

"Well, it certainly wasn't recorded on, like, an eight-track player or something."

"What?!" Johnny hollered again at the radio. "That does it!" He rolled onto his side and looked at Camden. "I'm never sleeping with her as long as I live!"

The fourth chapter, in which a new singer takes the stage, the chick magnet is stroked, tobacco sought, and bad vibes encountered

IN THE AUDIENCE that night a guy wearing psychedelic parachute pants shouted for Bill until, midway through the set, Sosdring pulled Lowery aside. "What's with this Bill? Why does that guy keep asking where Bill is?"

"It's an old Camper song," David said. "Just ignore him."

In high school David hung with a strange group—Bill Mc-Donald, David McDaniels—bright guys but alienated, both gifted and ashamed. It was a pathetic time to be young—impossible to endure really—when the only reported story was how well the hippies were tending their wounds (as they retreated from Weird Big Ideas to reexamine their values). The cultural target audience was twenty- and thirty-year-olds. Lowery had once heard that American teen suicide was at its height in those years. He could believe it. It felt like kids then had nothing to call their own, nothing that spoke to them but violence or whatever, so those normally smart enough to know better now whacked open Ko-nelco change machines and thrashed mailboxes and knifed tires and sprayed wretchedness across front lawns in antiperspirant.

Kids looking for an excuse found one—some formed bands, played loud music; Lowery and McDonald sneaked into the security lot that held the city's police cruisers and painted circle As on the sides of cop cars.

Also, Bill McDonald drummed—was one of the only drummers in town. Once, when they were loosely scheduled to jam at David McDaniels's parents' house, Bill failed to show. Furious, Lowery stomped around. "Where the hell is Bill?" he demanded. McDaniels strummed his guitar and repeatedly twanged, "Where, where the hell is Bill?" Lowery stepped to their little mike, motioned for McDaniels to continue, and began to suggest some humorous possibilities. They were throwaway lines really, that became a song, which became a Camper anthem. The manner in which it reclaimed trash culture apparently comforted some kids. Still, by now, David had done the song probably five thousand times. He had no desire to play it anymore, no matter how often it came requested.

It had become an oddly warm winter evening in Dallas. Following a very Pac-Man sunset—orange ball devours horizon, game over—the sky hovered as a smooth wash of blue, clear as a sigh but fading, the buildings of the city, their lights, seeming especially vivid in the dimming dusk. Hundreds—then thousands—of strolling folks were looking to take advantage of this unseasonably pleasant night. Because the stage sat in the club's front window, looky-loos stopped outside on the Deep Ellum sidewalk, watching the backs of the musicians and catching what they could of any sounds permeating the glass. There were groups of pals cruising the bars, couples exercising their pets, potential art buyers hopping around the galleries, middle-aged gentlemen wearing loafers and jeans with expensive satin jackets that had been tossed on over crummy T-shirts, and there were too loud kids fleeing drunkenly past, flinging out participles that dangled, then dissolved in the air behind them.

There were so few actually inside the club—thirty at the most—that David figured they might as well be on a first-name basis. "Everybody," he suggested, while replacing a broken string on his red Stratocaster, "I need a little time to get this new string on, so everybody in the room here, let's just go around and introduce ourselves, okay?" He pointed at a kid in a reversed baseball cap, untucked MISFITS T-shirt, hightops, and tube socks. "You first. Tell us your name."

The kid folded his arms. His expression did not change. He said nothing.

"All right then." David shrugged. "Somebody else start it."

"Where the hell is Bill?" the guy in psychedelic parachute pants hollered again.

"Look." David was winding the string and almost ready to go. "That's a whole 'nother band, okay? We aren't gonna do that song."

"Where the hell is Bill?"

"God. Shut up, man."

With Camper, it was like David always had to be on his best behavior. He had to pretend they were all good buds, had to say he adored only obscure music, had to toe a fucking party line on everything. Well, no more of that. From now on, he was telling the truth, always and forever—damn the consequences.

They got through three more songs before David stopped again to replace another broken string. Was it his fault guitar strings were such weak little motherfuckers? As he opened the tool kit and felt around for a replacement a familiar voice in the audience spoke up.

"Where the hell is Bill?"

"We'll only play it," Sosdring screamed, "if you sing it, Orca!"

"Yeah." David glared at this guy, who could not appreciate all their exertions on behalf of the new so now instead pathetically craved the safety of nostalgia. "You'll have to sing it, man. I'm sick to fucking death of it."

The guy shrugged—*whatever*—climbed up onstage, mugging for his friends, and took the mike with karaoke nonchalance.

"Shit," Pete murmured.

"Just A–D–E," Lowery explained. "Super slow." Johnny and Camden seemed to know the song. They dutifully began to play, but the guy in the psychedelic parachute pants drew a blank, couldn't sing. He blanched.

"What's the words?" he whispered into the microphone, pleading with David. "How's it start again?"

David shrugged, balefully indifferent, continued to cycle through the three chords, A–D–E, A–D–nauseam.

"Where the hell is Bill?" The audience snickered. The guy swallowed a few times. "Maybe, uh, he went to see . . . uh, Mariah Carey," he improvised. His friends clapped, urging him on. He smiled. "Whatever she sounds like, her hair seems scary." Pete tossed an exasperated gaze in Lowery's direction, whose expression remained hostile. More people hooted encouragement. "Maybe he went to call General Schwarzkopf . . . and tell him to please shoot his own nuts off!" More applause. The guy continued, bringing up Bill in the fashionable sideburns and corduroy of the Black Crowes, suggesting Teenage Mutant Ninja Turtles in Laura Ashley dresses had kidnapped Bill. He concluded with "Maybe he's recording as Vanilla Ice," which brought down the house. Before the applause died, Lowery stepped over. The guy beamed at him, stuck out a hand, assuming—apparently—that he would be congratulated. Instead, Lowery—tipped off by the bulge in the guy's shirt pocket—asked him for a cigarette. The guy obliged, and immediately the rest of the band descended to steal the pack.

Later, in a small office two doors in from the sound man's booth, David was getting paid by a man who seemed extraordinarily nervous.

"Where the hell is Bill?" inquired the man. "Heh, heh, heh. Some ovation."

"Yeah, it worked out pretty cool."

"Best rock and roll moment in club history, of all time—heh, heh," the nervous man said, wiping his brow, lighting a cigarette, and swigging some Miller, all in one smooth motion. "Oh, hey—" he went suddenly, then looked off, baffled, the way a cat will when smelling a ghost.

"David," Lowery reminded him.

"David, right. Hey man, how do you get your voice to sound like that?"

"My throat is just like covered in calluses by now, I've screamed it out so often, you know?"

"Heh, heh, heh. Cool, yeah." He handed across a wide stack of bills, mostly twenties and fifties, at least several thousand dollars thick. David unlocked his small silver briefcase, tucked the currency in an envelope—a glimpse of file folders and date books and copies of contracts, promoter and hotel info, the pager number for each club's sound man—before snapping the briefcase shut again.

He patted it lovingly. "We call this the chick magnet," Lowery said with pride.

"Heh, heh," said the nervous man. "Heh, heh, heh."

Having zeroed in on some tonnage, Pete, Johnny, and Camden stood poised near the door, each wearing a new special friend on his arm. They bade David farewell, pushed through the door and into Elm Street, where the too many people on their too many missions could now accurately be said to constitute one hellacious mob scene. It took but a few steps before Pete, Johnny, and Camden were swallowed up along with their special friends, and all six disappeared from sight.

Lowery went to the window, vaguely pissed. How would he get the chick magnet home? The foot traffic had spilled onto the street. Against his better instincts, he tried to depart and found himself overwhelmed, jostled from all sides. "There is this thing that happens when I am, as you say, 'asleep,' " David overheard one man tell another in a heavy Slavic accent. "I see pictures. Sometimes, they talk. People that I know show me things that I have done."

"Yes," his friend answered calmly. "Yes, that's what, our name for that, we call it: dreaming."

" 'Dreaming'? How curious it is, this 'dreaming'!"

"Hey," a low voice spoke. "Hey, you. David Lowery, of the much-vaunted musical rock band Camper Van Beethoven." David was unable to identify who'd spoken. He glanced around, a little frightened. The words had been put forth in that same sinister mash one hears when picking up a ringing pay phone—in the background children scream, some room in some house somewhere, while a voice dejectedly mutters across the line at you, seeking camaraderie. There were so many pedestrians, so many faces rushing up toward him. Lowery could scarcely turn. He felt like he was in an elevator or a packed public pool in the heat of summer.

"Hey you, you—David Lowery person!"

O Dallas, it occurred to him—*Ye heartland of assassinations, whose assassins assassinate one another in the news* . . .

David hesitated a step, fell back in retreat to the club. Tonight then, the others got the tonnage—but he got the money. Plus, thank God! it was good that he finally had some time to himself. He often thought admiringly of Greg Lisher, the shy guitarist in Camper, who so treasured time alone. Greg was always insisting he had to go "do some stuff" (stuff he never explained). *The mysterious Greg Lisher.* On tour it takes that kind of stubbornness just to get—at most—twenty minutes a day alone. There's always a meal or a packing or unpacking of gear that forces everyone back together. To get anywhere, to do anything, they need one another. "It's like we're on Boy Island or something," Sosdring joked, more than once. The day is motel, minivan, restaurant, minivan, restaurant, minivan, club, minivan, motel, minivan, restaurant, minivan, club, minivan, motel. Sleep and repeat.

Yes, David agreed with Greg. It was nice to be alone for a moment.

Still, this was not to excuse what Greg had done a year ago, too worried about overloading and burning out to adequately weigh the financial straits Camper Van Beethoven were in, disregarding Lowery's advice and instead siding with the others that Camper should disband just eight shows from the end, in Sundsvall, Sweden. "If we quit now," Lowery warned him, "we lose fourteen thousand outright in costs, ten thousand of our tour support. The company loaned us three hundred and fifty to make *Key Lime*!" Virgin later failed to relinquish control of the publishing royalties, which might have covered some of these losses.

David felt drained. He took a seat on a bar stool. The bartender brought him a Miller and some matches. He constructed himself a cigarette, pulled a match from the book, struck it to life. That was a good smell, the burnt sulfur. David's eyes went to the track lighting, the plastic decorations, the fake plants. He smoked half the cigarette while reading the names of the liquor bottles behind the bar. He ran a hand through his hair and looked out front again.

Although the flood of people had crested and peaked, young people continued to circulate through the streets, handsome women in various stages of undress, in black bras and white slacks, their boyfriends dressed in open, floppy shirts and post-hippie regalia. Teenagers staggered around handcuffed together, wearing nearly nothing but ecstatic smiles. Inside a squad car parked in the center of Elm two cops seemed engrossed with the door of the club. The doorman attempted to engage them in upbeat chatter while throwing customers out into the street. The bartender upended trash cans of beer bottles into the dumpster; the waitresses smoked and sighed.

Lowery took it all in, protectively stroked the chick magnet. Why hadn't he placed these proceeds in the hotel safe? He had to learn to overcome this suspicion, or one night he'd lose every cent amid some rabble-filled scene such as this.

Lowery had certainly learned the hard way—the money isn't in sales of recordings, nor airplay, nor soundtracks. All those dollars, in one way or another, essentially find themselves funneled back to the company. Those markets exist to make possible a band's sole source of true revenue: live shows. And so that's what David would do now—he'd tour this band endlessly and record . . . enough.

"Want me to call you a cab?" volunteered the club's bouncer. "It's these damn kids, they never go to bed."

"A cabbie," Lowery wanted to know, "he could drive through this mess?"

"Oh sure! They're trained professionals."

"What is it, about six dollars, six-fifty? We're staying at the Aristocrat."

"Given the state of things, I'd say maybe more like ten."

David winced. Okay, inside the chick magnet now was over $9,000—the profits from Tucson (350 capacity), Austin (700 capacity), and Dallas (300 capacity)—but really, $9,000 wasn't as much as it sounded either, when you were on tour. The band got the door (against a minimum guarantee), drink tickets, deli trays, dinner, and usually free lodging and souvenir merchandise from the club. A few extra dollars came nightly from T-shirt sales. Each musician was given a small per diem, and the rest had to be available to tip tech personnel or to pay for phone calls and gasoline, oil changes, and fax charges.

"Yeah, okay then," David said, grudgingly accepting the

bouncer's offer. He went to the motel, slept, and the next day it started again—minivan, restaurant, minivan, restaurant, minivan. . . .

SOME ways down the road, they got to the next club. But this time, after sound check, the band drove in search of tobacco. There was a palpable air of mischief about; this marked the very first time they had smoked their way through an entire packet of loose tobacco. Pete looked naughtily pleased with himself.

"I'm broadcasting from a U.S. airbase somewhere in Saudi Arabia," said the radio.

Hickman glanced up and flashed his bright billboard smile, momentarily blinding David.

"Man we got"—he addressed Lowery, as if David didn't already know—"tonnage!"

They went from market to market in quest of their beloved Drum tobacco ("Accept no substitutes!" Pete Sosdring kept fervently declaring), and Johnny proceeded to tell more than David wanted to hear about the sexual exploits at the Aristocrat Hotel.

A session of strip pinochle ("strippy knuckle," the girls had called it) had degenerated into a spanking free-for-all until Johnny hauled his special friend off into the bathroom, while Pete lowered his onto the bedroom carpet and positioned himself upon her. This left both beds open for Camden and his girl.

Camden was now on the scoreboard after joining this quasi beating-cum-orgy: He had racked up 130 points—except there was an asterisk beside his score (*how Roger Maris!*). Camden had been interrupted before completing the sex act, and so these were, as Pete haughtily reminded everyone, "pity points."

"I didn't know it was a race," Camden protested feebly. He saw himself as penalized for moving atop his special friend at too sensual a pace. "I'm just getting started when all of a sudden Johnny comes crashing out of the bathroom zipping up his fly, and Pete pops up, says he's through. The girls are chased running out the door—literally chased—with Pete slapping at their behinds with a belt. I had no idea we were even racing."

"Hey, if it moves, fuck it," said Pete coldly.

Lowery chuckled. "The Roadie Code, that's right. 'If it moves, fuck it. If it doesn't move, then load it in the van and fuck it later.' "

" 'If it's white, snort it,' " Hickman happily chimed in. " 'If it's green, smoke it.' "

"And there's one other," Lowery strained to recall. "What is it again?"

" 'If it's got long hair,' " answered Pete without a pause, " 'Put a guitar on it.' "

"The Saudis," said the radio, "have taken to calling the F-117 Stealth fighters *shabai*. Which means 'the ghost.' "

Camden tried to tell them about this nice photographer he met at breakfast named Carrie Mae who'd been reading Isak Dinesen but all Pete wanted to know was what she looked like, how much she weighed, and whether she had pendulous breasts or small, pointy ones.

Carrie Mae had told Camden of the wildflowers that ran along the highway in springtime: the red ones called Indian paint-

brushes, the yellow called fiddlesticks, the blue called bluebonnets; and she explained that it was a tradition for Texans to drive
their children out to the nearest field of bluebonnets, plop them
down in the middle, and snap their photos.

"Doesn't that sound weird?" Camden asked the others.

Johnny shrugged good-naturedly.

"So then you fucked her," proposed Pete. In his eyes there
was nothing whatsoever. "Just wake me when you get to that
part."

"You know," said Johnny, "I read about a Carrie Mae once, a
murderess—"

"Different one," Camden interjected.

"She killed fifteen children before they caught up with her."

"Johnny," David explained, "has this special appetite for mur-
derers."

"I was supposed to be a detective," said Johnny. "I would be,
if I wasn't a musician. A lot of policemen used to come to my
wife's salon and I'd wash, cut, and style their hair. They'd tell me
all about the cases they were working on, let me read the files,
show me pictures of suspects and handwriting samples, and I'd
give them my hunches. And I was always right. I mean, I still
think Wayne B. Williams should go free. You remember the guy
who murdered twenty-eight young Atlanta blacks around 1980?
Wayne B. Williams is not that guy. Convicted on circumstantial
evidence, a few fibers pulled out of the river. They got the wrong
man, the pattern is just not right. I told everyone they should be
looking for a white man, quiet, methodical, the product of a
broken home. That's the pathology I'd suspect."

"But none of those fuckers would listen," lamented David.

"Nobody listened!" Hickman cried, feigning hysteria. "Nobody at all!"

The minivan limped around in confused circles, stopping anywhere that appeared a likely outlet for the finest in loose tobacco. They could not find their favored brand. Desperation led David to make abrupt swings of the steering wheel whenever anyplace so much as hinted at sin.

The difficulty of it put David in a bad mood. The city appeared like a tall obstacle in the roadway, all McDonald's and smogged-in skyscrapers, rising cruel and petty in the late-day haze. Car alarms sounded like busy signals, sirens like cackling monkeys. Welcome back everybody to Boy Island, David thought.

"Look at her." Johnny motioned toward a nifty lady who'd accelerated her Taurus up alongside them. She had corvette-red nails, a small gold necklace. "A hundred twenty-five pounds!" He tried to catch her attention.

"No doubt lured to us by the chick magnet," went David.

"But seriously," said Johnny. "Where's a woman that decked-out headed at this hour?"

"I don't know, Detective Hickman," replied Lowery. "Whyn't you tell us?"

"Not to or from the office, not at this hour. Not going to school or a show, not dressed like that."

Pete sullenly okayed these points.

"Which leaves only this," Johnny declared. "That she is driving to someone's hotel room to strip. There might be music involved, a tape player, her dancing to it naked while this person watches."

"C'mon Johnny," growled Lowery.

"Think about it," said Hickman. "Where *else* could she be going?"

"To the . . . the . . . hmmm. Wow. I suppose you're right."

Camden shifted, as if intending to contribute something to the conversation, but did not follow through.

"He's getting that look again." Pete indicated Camden. "Like we beat him too much."

At the next stoplight David turned in his seat, gave Camden a puzzled glance. An unhealthful air quality hovered around him, in his wounded, downcast mouth. "Were you hit with a tranquilizer dart, man? What are you, bleeding internally?"

"You okay?" Johnny asked. He sounded sincere.

Camden moaned, as if summoning up his final strength. "I just don't feel well," he went at last. They leaned back.

"The Iraqis," said the radio, "have parked MIG-21 aircraft near the ziggurat ruins in Ur, knowing the Allies will not bomb the cradle of civilization."

THEIR fifteenth or twentieth stop was a Holiday Inn that advertised an adjacent dime store. It was getting late. They waited in the minivan while David went inside. David warned them he was going to purchase whatever tobacco the place had so they could start back to the club.

He pushed his way into the dime store. The electric eye sang its song. David was still carrying the chick magnet. By now, he'd grown so attached to it that Johnny's suggestion about cuffing the case to David's wrist no longer amused anyone; they might as well, David agreed. He turned right, down an aisle of hunting vests, crossed to a counter. There were only a few other customers, youngsters in bandannas standing near the soda coolers, tossing Lemonheads into one another's mouths and flipping off the surveillance camera. David was underwhelmed by their predictably vulgar gestures. Behind the counter, he saw blank cassette tapes, packages of batteries, toiletries for sale. They kept tobacco locked inside a plastic case. David set the chick magnet on the counter and awaited a salesclerk.

Camden had him worried. They'd really pegged the kid wrong. Of course, Camden had been a great drummer at first, that hadn't purely been their imagination. Well, so maybe just he, Johnny, and Pete would hire a new drummer each tour. Could hire a bassist, too, if Pete grew uninterested. Like with Camper; by the end, they had not only "band members"—Victor, Crispy, Lisher—but "hired musicians"—Morgan, Immergluck—as well. The latter were infinitely less complicated to maintain—no split, no percentage headaches, just a flat performance fee, a set per diem—and such simplicity appealed to Lowery. A band of employees—*such low overhead, man, if only*! Hire a drummer, hire a bassist; it'd be like, you know, just dating a rhythm section rather than marrying them.

I mean, David thought, you go see the Coasters or the Lettermen or the Spinners or the Ronettes nowadays and what do you get? You get the famous old-time pop hits, yes, but not performed by any famous old-timers. They're all at home collecting royalties. You don't see the band's original members, they've long since sold their roles in the band to some hacks with a great deal of dough who always wanted to be onstage doing these songs;

those hacks, in turn, have long since auctioned off their memberships, too, after a few years of being in their dream band. There was no band too mighty that it wouldn't degenerate into a community college stageplay of itself, as the show *Beatlemania* did for the Beatles.

A security guard came over to help David. Naturally, the store didn't sell their beloved Drum. David no longer cared. He bought what they had and left.

"Nope," David reported to his bandmates, "they didn't have it." He tossed anonymous packages of bargain-priced tobacco at everyone.

"Arrgggghhhhh!" squealed Pete Sosdring, hurling his package back at David as if it were some feral rat. "I am pissed, &tc., thank you!"

"This is really pitiful," grieved Camden, idly fingering a package that bore the brand name Safe Choice Tobacco.

Hickman worked to put an optimistic spin on it. "I got this real good feeling about Baton Rouge."

"Driver," Pete commanded in an awful accent. "Back to the club! Now! We must to the rock and roll."

"I'm trying, I'm trying," said David, taking random rights and lefts.

"Don't tell me we're lost," requested Johnny.

"No. Yes. Not really."

"That's a relief."

"Nobody's ever as lost as they think. Or, I also think, everybody is just equally lost. You know? Hey, you guys ever play 'Honk at Insects'?"

Pete narrowed his eyes in suspicion. "Are you changing the subject?"

"See that one." David began tooting the horn wildly. "A whole swarm."

"I didn't see anything," Camden answered.

Pete issued a restless sound from deep in his throat.

"There's another." David honked twice. "And another."

"I don't buy it," said Johnny. "I'd say we're lost."

"There's also, 'Honk 'n' Wave for No Reason at All.' Look."

David pointed out an elderly couple. They appeared almost gray. The man wore nurse's shoes, walked with the help of a cane. The woman dragged a cart containing a few groceries. Hurrying to make it home before dark, their steps were small and stuttering. They paused on a nearby walkway to catch their breath, leaning on a tall terra-cotta bucket that brimmed with dead geraniums. They both wore hats from the forties, long colorless coats.

"Everyone turn and face those people there. And when I honk, everyone wave."

The horn beeped. The old couple dropped their arms and inched slowly around until they could make out four boys in a Dodge minivan, all grinning and waving madly at them. Nervously they studied the minivan. In an erratic, palsied fashion they put on bifocals, squinted at the minivan some more. Then, apparently, they recognized the boys. Their faces lit up. They happily waved back.

The minivan sped off.

The next left was Washington. The address of the club was

5913 Washington. They turned out to be only a few miles from the club. Everything now looked familiar, the refineries, the cement churches with tall barred windows, the dilapidated electronics store, the sidewalks piled with spools of rusty wire, corn husks, and torn-up gizmos and gadgetry.

"See?" said David confidently. "And y'all thought we were lost."

"Tonight a SCUD slipped past the Patriot system lent to Israel," said the radio. "Seventy in Tel Aviv were injured. Three Israelis were found dead from heart attacks."

"Be warned," went David. "Fatty foods taken in combination with crazed dictators may be hazardous to one's cardiovascular system."

"During these times of national crisis," said Johnny, "please people, *watch your cholesterol.*"

"You know," Camden said. "This Carrie Mae woman—"

"One-hundred-and-twenty-pound Carrie Mae?" Pete snarled.

"Yeah. Well, like I said, she's a photographer. She went to Mexico to photograph this Indian tribe and almost immediately she began to have these dreams in which, by photographing them, she was cutting off their faces and devouring their souls. She had to return home right away."

David laughed. "They were bad-vibing her, man."

"And David would know," said Johnny proudly.

"Yeah. I can do it to anyone, anytime I want. In Camper I used to always, like, bad-vibe Morgan, and she'd totally freak. And I remember even in, like, high school, there was this guy I always hated, what a total fucker. And I started bad-vibing him by doing this thing—I still do it to him every so often—where I would write to newspapers all over the country, I'd write letters to the editor, and they'd be full of all these completely over-the-top theories about Nazis and UFOs and shit, and I'd sign the guy's name to these letters."

"Your friend from high school?" Camden asked.

"Not my friend, but yeah. So that if the guy ever tries to run for office or get a government job or whatever, all these letters of his will surface with all these very deranged, wacked-out beliefs in them."

"Land offensive expected at any time," said the radio.

Dusk fell across Texas. The air was sticky and felt like glue. The sky was orange as cheese puffs, the trees as stale as pretzel sticks.

"We are talking bad vibes here," intoned Pete soberly. "Most definitely."

The fifth chapter, in which David tears up the set list, Johnny becomes uncharacteristically cross, Pete gets a woody, and Camden encounters the memory of something unexpected at a party

THE VENUE WAS an abandoned film theater made of cinder blocks, covered in graffiti ("FUCK Y'ALL we're from TEXAS," "Ninth Day Underground," "The FUNK'S in the HOUSE get HIP to it"), dark, oversize, and filled—as far as Camden could see—with rows of bolted-down, rotting movie seats.

When someone in the crowd yelled up to ask what Hickman's green shorts were made of, Lowery fielded the question. "I'll tell you, I'll tell you. And you can believe me 'cause I only tell the truth now. That's what we're all about, we tell the truth—not like my old band.

"His shorts are silk. And last night, Johnny was, like, whipped with a belt by three sorority girls, and so, like, beneath those shorts he's got these big, red welt marks on his ass."

Camden was set upon the club's ridiculous drummer pedestal. He recalled how, before coming out onstage, Johnny checked the mirror to make sure he had no lingering bruises from the night before. Camden was amazed that David's pledge of honesty was so nonchalantly broken. The girls in question were not sorority girls at all.

In the audience Camden saw those by now familiar signs of Orca distress—grimaces from innocent faces, anguished looks peering out from beneath tie-dyed knit caps. But they could not have known that the lead singer had so quickly and absolutely betrayed his vow of truthfulness; rather, they were probably concerned that David Lowery, whom they had come to know as that sweet hippie in that sweet hippie band from that sweet hippie town in California, had just forced speculation about the ass of the handsome guitarist standing next to him.

Five songs in Lowery tore up the set list and sprinkled the audience with the pieces. He suddenly decided that they would play something they'd practiced only once, a deathly slow number called "Lullaby." It seemed to Camden that the song took forever. By show's end Lowery was without his shirt and three times had warned the crowd that he was about to lock the doors and lick each of their bodies.

Afterward, as he disassembled his kit, Camden worried whether the audience was getting what it paid for. Or were they disturbed, bothered that this David Lowery music was not kind and cuddlesome like Camper Van Beethoven? This guy used to be older, they're probably thinking; they didn't pay good money to see this guy's eyes go black and gleam this nasty way, to hear him sing (as he did every night) "Happy birthday baby to *me*." Few songs were familiar. The players were new. The aim was alienating. Though almost certainly they experienced traditionally great music—pacing was tight, the playing professional, the voices worked hard—a few intriguing lines always sneaked through the clogged and murky club mixes, enticing snatches— still few listeners at the time could yet figure how this sound was at all important, particularly from Lowery, who before—as their favored budding songwriter—had seemed capable of much greater complexity.

Some part of his mind argued back that it wasn't as lousy as all that; but mostly Camden avoided visiting that part of his mind when he was tired. He slid cymbals into the equipment bag and wearily closed the snare in its case. Lately he was always tired— had been tired, it felt like, for years and years. Show him to a flat surface—a mattress, a table, an incline, a backseat, anything— and he'd lie on it for hours without moving. He did not dream as he slept and in truth did not even sleep so much as lie with eyes shut, wishing he were sleeping, wishing he were dreaming, in which case he'd dream of being home with his mom on a sick day with a heating pad and a bowl of soup, playing checkers. But he wasn't home, wasn't even asleep, but only somewhere in Texas faking it.

THEY were behind the building after the show, loading the mini-van, when a towering, raven-haired teenager stepped in front of David. She wore bib overalls and too much mascara. She was closely trailed by another girl and two guys.

"Hi," she spoke with great emphasis.

David stopped in his tracks, his arms wrapped around a very heavy guitar amplifier with a Music Man logo on its side.

"Hi," he said back. Camden saw him examining her, looking

past the bib overalls to appraise her bulk, her high shoulders, her deep chest, her tall legs, delighted at her size.

"Remember me?"

"Sure," he said matter-of-factly.

"You do, for reals?" She turned to her friends, tightened her expression. "I told you he would!"

"I can't recall your name."

She touched his hand understandingly, as if to convey that this was a common problem for her, then told him, "Tanja. Spelled with a J and an A at the end. T-A-N-J-A."

"Tanja! Right, right."

"I'm Alicen," went the other girl. "It's spelled with one L and C-E-N."

"What?"

"A-L-I-C-E-N."

"Okay, good."

"And this is George and Brad."

"How's it going?" David shook their hands. "I think I can manage the spelling on those last two. So." He turned back to Tanja. "What's going on?"

"I wanted to see if you meant what you said."

"What?"

"You don't remember? I met you at that party, you remember, at that guy's house? Last year? You remember you told me, remember what you told me?"

"Yeah. No, I remember you, I just. What did I say?"

She pressed her right breast into his shoulder, leaned in to whisper something.

"Wow. I said that? I'm sorry, I guess." David shrugged. "So would you mind if I asked a slightly personal question?"

"Not at all."

"Exactly how much do you weigh?"

A few minutes later the band watched David follow Tanja and her friends out to a black Volkswagen Cabriolet convertible. Sosdring returned to directing the intricate ballet of boxes and cases and bags which was the loading up of the back of their vehicle. The minivan's rear three-foot-by-five-foot space had to accommodate all of their equipment. They had refined, through trial and error, the best approach for collapsing this stuff: Begin with the amplifiers, then the drums, then the other instruments. Then look for holes to plug with "love"—a phrase that to Pete meant anything easy and without problems, and in this case was an abbreviation for "the love box," a crate of cords and pedals that was always light in the loading and obligingly fit most any-where. There was also "the death case," a weighty and trouble-some trunk, always bigger than it seemed, that eventually had to be fitted in somewhere. Then there was the chick magnet, the trash bags full of Camper T-shirts, everyone's suitcases and travel bags, cases of Miller given to them by the club, their individual sacks of tobacco, and whatever paperbacks they happened to be reading.

"Everything in?"

It was Lowery asking. The Cabriolet had driven him over.

"Yeah," Pete said.

"Seems to be," said Johnny.

David nodded. "Cool. I'm going to the party in their car. You guys follow."

"A party? Who says?"

David jerked a thumb at the black Volkswagen. "They're throwing us a party."

For a few moments, no one said anything.

"I thought," said Johnny, uncharacteristically cross, "we were heading out right now."

"It's not like we have hotel reservations anywhere."

"What about the Riverland Suites Motel in Baton Rouge?"

"Let's check out this party first."

"There gonna be girls there?" asked Johnny, still frowning.

"Yeah."

"I mean other girls, not just your big special friend there."

"Yeah."

"You got this confirmed?"

"Yeah."

Johnny raised his shoulders, acquiesced. "All right."

"I'd rather get going," Pete spoke up. "It's already midnight."

"Me, too," went Camden.

David ignored them, returned to the other car. The kids in the Volkswagen had put their top down. David climbed into the backseat alongside Tanja.

They got into the minivan, Johnny and Pete in front, Camden in back. As they followed the Volkswagen, tailgating through the city, David and Tanja were posed squarely in the headlight beams, smoking and throwing their heads back every so often to exhale great bursts of uproarious laughter.

"Ha. Ha. Ha," said Johnny sourly. "Oh, David, you are so terribly funny."

"This'll be a complete washout," predicted Pete. He seemed heartened by Hickman's bad mood.

Tanja was perched a few feet away from David, who sat himself upright, stretching his arm, easing within reach of her shoulder.

"How old is this girl?" Johnny asked.

"About two in dog years," Pete blandly replied. "But she's smarter than your av-er-age gummy bear."

Johnny shook his head. "No way is he ever gonna unsnap those overalls."

"This," Pete summed up, "blows."

"No way will she put out. Abso-fucking-lutely no way."

"A party, yeah, fun," griped Pete. "Not!"

They continued to focus on David Lowery as, ahead of them, he charmed his special friend in his chauffeured Volkswagen. The lighting made it seem a cross between a movie premiere and a prom.

Johnny popped the glove compartment, pulled out a comb, and worked, as he drove, to make himself presentable for the party. Pete, on the other hand, picked his nose for a full minute and then burped wetly.

"You know man, I thought it was a cool show," said Johnny, relaxing behind the wheel.

"I think we shocked a few Orcas," said Pete. "I know I was getting a woody out there on that last one. It was like I had a fucking glazed donut in my BVDs, man."

Pete and Johnny had taken to performing the encores in their underwear. Although Camden'd noticed Pete's eyes shut during the final number, he'd had no idea the bass had hidden an erection.

"A bear claw, more like it," commented Johnny, seeking the most precise comparison. "Or a fucking maple bar."

"It was so mad. I had the back of the instrument just leaned up against it, rubbing it all slow. Fuck. This is the tour," Pete swore, as he had many times already. "The tour I should've done when I was eighteen, man."

The "party" was located in the upstairs of some split-level, off-campus housing. There were four bedrooms, a common living room/dining room area, and a kitchenette with a small stove. A vast tapestry painted with the likeness of a handsome, slick-haired rock and roll star dominated the wall of the main room. A junked-out sofa and several sticks of thrift-store furniture were strewn beneath the tapestry.

Lowery put on a compact disc entitled *A Different Kind of Tension* and some boy named Eugenia interrogated the band about pasta—"Does everybody want righetti? Would that be good? Righetti, hmmm?"

David started telling how Camper had covered another song by this same band, a song called "Harmony in My Head."

The girl named Alicen ambled past, pausing long enough to equip each of them with an unrefrigerated bottle of Miller.

"Ah! The syrupy joy, the sweet yellow of Miller!" declared Sosdring with a rare enthusiasm. "Nectar of urinals!"

"Long may it rain!" Hickman heartily agreed. "Who amongst those congregated here tonight dares resist the Kennedy of beers, a lure bobbing in the waters of Chappaquiddick?! To Miller!!"

"Amen." Pete toasted him.

"Amen." David took a beer, pointed at the disc player, asked the boy named George—"Remember when this came out? I was like, fucking digging it. Home from college, working nights at the newspaper, taking lots of speed."

"What year did this come out?"

"I think it was '79."

"Nineteen *seventy-nine?*" George sipped his warm Miller. "In 1979, I was five years old! There were four hundred million fewer human beings on this planet in those days!"

"Holy shit," Pete Sosdring softly muttered.

"Okay," said Eugenia from the kitchenette. "Does everybody still want righetti?"

"Yeah."

"Definitely."

"I could care."

"Sounds great."

"How many times you gonna ask?"

"I just need a real good count here. We're gonna run to the store a second, then we'll be right back. We just need to count how many mouths we're feeding here."

Brad raised his voice to explain what was "so crucial" about this group named the Buzzcocks, how you had here "the origin" of some "underrated, much maligned" musical group called Magazine and "perhaps more critically still, the ground source for that phenomenally significant hetero-homo culture leap found in Pete Shelley's solo work."

The band sounded like gaunt, pucker-faced brats to Camden.

Sandwiched between the speakers, all he noticed of this CD were the band's thin, whiny British voices.

Pete Sosdring glared about the room. "Nothing like loud music," he sneered at Hickman, "with some college boy screaming why 'this is so great,' explaining it all like I was deaf like Helen Keller."

"The Camper legacy, man." Johnny shrugged. This did not bother him terribly much. "They were such a total rock critic's band."

Pete contemptuously shook his head. "Fuck that."

The Miller executed its responsibilities.

"I can't feel the future," the compact disc diligently informed everyone. "And I'm not even certain that there is a past."

"You know," Brad said to Camden, avoiding the temptation to reply directly to the stereo. "If this song was slowed down just a little it could sound like that song you guys do, 'Don't Fuck Me Up.'"

Camden cocked his head, listening. "Yeah."

"I believe in the workers' revolution," David crooned along to the CD. "I believe in the final solution, I believe in the elixir of youth, I believe in the absolute truth; there is no love in this world anymore."

"I remember in Richmond," Camden told Brad, "I asked David what 'Don't Fuck Me Up' was about. He'd just written it and he came in, goes, 'I got this song.' So we were just jamming on it and stuff. And I could hear some of the words he was singing and so I go, 'What's it about?' And he goes, 'You know, it's like when you're sixteen and you're really really drunk as hell at a party and you're just really pissed off at everybody and you want to kick the door down and you're angry because your girlfriend broke up with you or something. . . . It's about that.' Well."

The entire party consisted of them and three guys and three girls. Tanja and George and Alicen and Brad were of the Black Volkswagen convertible contingent, Jenny and Eugenia were new. They had not attended the show; they spoke of having midterms to prepare for. Jenny was lanky and angular with eyes that were large, brown, and alert. She smiled easily but maintained about her a sense of distance, as if she were only so present at this party, as if there were other unaddressed reasons she had not joined the others in going that night to see David Lowery's new band. She seemed both flattered and irritated that the rock band had come home with her roommates, that they were now piled about her living quarters when she had tests to study for. Yet she was receptive and not at all unpleasant. She was famished, having been—as she informed them—all evening with Eugenia cramming at the library.

As they arrived, Eugenia was already standing at the stove, pulling out pots and pans to start a meal for everyone. Eugenia, too, was tall, with a round and handsome face. He had deep dimples, rosy cheeks, flopped-forward hair, and lips so dark—like bruised plums they appeared against his pale skin—that they seemed almost to lift away from him, as if posing an inquiry to the rest of his features.

Eugenia wore a button-down collared shirt untucked at the waist. The corner of the shirt collar nearest the throat was creased back, and apparently this was intentional, because every so often Eugenia would check to make sure it was still folded that way. He would be doing something like filling the pot to boil water, stacking plates, washing some silverware, pulling paper towels to fold as napkins, something like that, when absently his finger would tap the top of his chest, his mouth would gasp in remembrance, his eyes would turn to peer searchingly into some reflective surface (a nearby teapot, say, or the kitchen window), his hand would curl the collar corner down once more, and his lips would let go a dramatic sigh. Watching from across the room, from where he sat on the sofa, Camden was unable to make sense out of this. Was this folded collar his attempt to cover an embarrassing love-bite? Was Eugenia simply anxious to ensure that the prominent bone along his collar—his strikingly frail clavicle—be permanently on full display? Did he register the vanity of his own gesture, the way Camden could not help but notice as time and again Eugenia sought out his own reflection, released a tender expulsion of breath, ever so small, slightly edgy yet satisfied?

Eugenia did nothing for Camden but raise questions.

"The essence of being, these feelings I'm feeling," observed the Buzzcocks. "I just want them to last."

But the most significant question in the air, audible to the bandmates if not to these youngsters, was whether or not David Lowery was headed toward getting laid. If he was, then this raised a secondary concern in its wake—namely, which of the remaining two girls went with these three particular guys, who among these females was "taken" versus who was available?

"I believe what I believe in, and I believe in. Yes, I believe in."

The first they saw of Jenny—the scholar—she was whispering to Alicen at the head of the hallway that led to the bedrooms.

As she whispered, she leaned in quite close, their heads nearly touching, and clasped Alicen's hand. Upon finishing the two of them appeared—in the dimness of the corner—to be either hugging or possibly even kissing. Of course, Jenny also sat very near to George through the meal, playfully tousling his hair, so no one could be certain of her preference or availability.

"There is no love in this world anymore."

Alicen was the least showy of the three girls. Time and again, Pete or Johnny would pay Alicen some attention but within moments drift away, their interest evaporating that fast. Perhaps it was simply her minuscule height or her puny weight: She was of such insignificant poundage that probably no one could see enacting the logistical complications of a one-night stand with a twenty-year-old simply to add ninety or ninety-five points to their tonnage score. As the game stood that night, it was really David Lowery who needed to add to his score (he was now scarcely ahead of Camden after last night's pity points), and David had focused all his efforts on Tanja de Mascara.

"Poor Iraqis," Tanja sniffed.

"Yeah," David mumbled.

"It's like," Brad said. "We have Tomahawk Cruise Missiles, Patriot air defense weapons, Titans and Minutemen, Hawks and Sparrows and Sidewinders and Mavericks, F-117 Stealth Fighters, F-15E Strike Eagles, F-16 Falcons, and F-111 fighter-bombers, Taloses and Aegises, Sea Sparrows, Tartars, Terriers, Harpoons, Stingers, Pershings, Rapiers, Chaparral, Rolands, Hellfires, Lipscomb, Narwhals, Sturgeons, Threshers, and Skipjacks. . . . And what do they have? Scuds. That's it. 'Scud.' One syllable, sounds like 'dud.'"

"Poor Iraqis," Tanja sniffed again.

"Yeah," David mumbled again.

One of the Buzzcocks interrupted with something to the effect of how he believed in the things he'd never had—in his Mom and his Dad—and he observed once again that there was no longer any love in this world, and he then stressed this observation several more times.

"Yeah, Pete," David began prompting the vocalist. "Get up there. C'mon, Pete."

And as if on cue, the vocalist began to climb: "There is no love in this world anymoooooooore. There is no love in this world anymoooooooore."

"Who is this singing?" asked George.

"Pete Shelley," answered David.

"What's he do now?"

"Isn't it true he's gay?" asked Johnny, perhaps believing that this was a full-time job.

"Oh?" chirped Eugenia, his interest piqued. Camden blushed, tried not to stare at his bared collarbone.

"One time in London," David said, "Pete Shelley came and saw Camper play. Afterward, he invited me back to his hotel room."

"Wow," breathed Eugenia.

"Man, I shoulda gone, you know."

"Oh." Eugenia nodded. "You should have."

"I mean," David addressed everybody with a depraved chuckle. "It *was* Pete Shelley!"

Everyone laughed along.

For some reason, Eugenia's giggle made Camden nostalgic for, of all things, his brother. Camden was just so melancholy, that was the thing, ill and melancholy. Somehow that expressed itself in feelings of nostalgia. His brother too had been exquisite to behold—had possessed, like Eugenia, a sense of nobility, an unreluctant sunniness.

"Hey, did you guys know," David then queried the party, "that Pete was on *Soul Train* when he was thirteen?"

"No way!" went Tanja vacantly.

"*Soul Train* . . ." Alicen said. "That's . . . ? What is that again?"

"A television show," answered David.

"Oh. Really? Oh. Wild. When was this?"

Pete Sosdring looked at her. "It was . . ." He paused. "Just some show."

"Really?" Alicen showed him a bland smile. "So I hope you don't mind me asking, but how old are you guys?"

"Twenty-six," answered Pete hastily. "All of us. Except Camden."

"Twenty-six. That's not so old, not really."

"There is! no love! in this! world any! moooore!"

"So this," Pete said, with all the charm he could muster, "seems like a pretty fucked-up place; Austin, I mean."

"—Houston. Um, yeah," agreed Alicen. "It's pretty yucky."

"The whole city government is all, like, corrupt," George said. "And the police chief is a woman."

"And now she's pregnant," said Alicen.

"Your chief of police is pregnant?" Lowery snickered. "Crazy shit."

"Oh, how terribly bizarre," droned Pete, slouched low in his chair and thoroughly uncivil. "My, my. The chief of police of Austin is pregnant."

"Houston," Tanja reminded him. "We're in Houston. This," she gestured without respect at the front window, "is Houston."

"Are they serious?" asked Camden distressedly. "What happened to Austin? Was Austin last night?"

"I guess so," Johnny said. He frowned, solemnly bit at a cuticle.

Eugenia smiled lewdly at Camden.

They sat in silence for a time, gulping warm Miller and ignoring Pete Shelley as he sang himself hoarse.

"There is! uh no! uh love! uh in! uh this! uh world! uh any . . . MOOOOOOOORE!"

The band—impatient, sweaty, and tired from the show—was eager (all but the singer/songwriter) to resolve something one way or the other so they could sleep. Periodically Pete pulled Johnny aside and pressured him into approaching David to find out if they would be leaving anytime soon. Such pestering clearly aggravated David.

And louder and louder grew the unasked question—with their fascinated, wide eyes and their laughing, open mouths, were these Houston girls interested in screwing somebody or were they simply turned-on to hear (firsthand) the stories of musicians who once were famous and (who knows?) one day soon might be again?

"Well, you know," Pete Sosdring stood, addressing everyone in the room, "we have to get all the way to Baton Rouge, Louisiana, by morning."

Nobody appeared to hear for, just then, Eugenia stepped from the kitchen, his arms laden with dinner. And the food was served—overcooked, watery righetti slipping around on paper plates beneath a thin patina of half-melted Velveeta.

They did their best to clean their plates but about the nicest compliment anyone could muster was, "Oh."

After dinner, Eugenia drew Camden to his room. "I want to show you something." They ended up sitting side-by-side on the edge of a futon, beside a tall floor lamp with a ruffled shade. There was a table in the corner, covered in library books, and a cassette player on a nightstand.

Camden felt very light-headed. "What."

"Can I hold your hand?"

Camden recalled sitting near his weakening brother, stroking his brother's splendid hands, so slender and pale, and petting his face with a delicate cloth. "I don't think you should." Eugenia did anyway and the light-headedness retreated back to where it came from. Camden thanked him, then admitted he felt weird about this.

"So . . . Camden . . . where are you from?"

"L.A.," Camden lied.

"Originally, I mean."

"L.A."

"I never knew people actually came from California. I never met anyone who was actually from there."

"Yep."

"Is that nice?"

"I guess so."

"I imagine it's pretty tolerant out there, hunh?"

"Yep," Camden began, but then rethinking his lie he launched into the story of his former boss Mr. Schuck, perhaps the least tolerant man on the face of the earth.

Eugenia interrupted him. "I meant tolerant, like in, you know. . . . Like the police here, they know me pretty well and they pull me over all the time, you know, because of what I'm into. I just wondered if that's standard practice everywhere with people who're into an 'alternative lifestyle' or . . ."

"Yeah?"

"It is?"

"I don't know," Camden answered.

"Let me ask you a question—what, are you laughing at me?"

"All you do is ask questions!"

Eugenia rocked with laughter. "All right, here it is: You like boys, right?"

"Ah, it's so . . . I mean, it's funny you ask that because I keep thinking how I don't understand these guys, you know, the guys in the band, so often I can't even tell what we're talking about. On the other hand, I mean, I loved my brother. I really miss him. I think I understood him better maybe than I do girls."

"Yeah. Me, too."

Camden's brother had indeed been gorgeous, had even died marvelously, from his own blood having turned bad. It made no sense to them; it was like watching a statue fall apart. Camden was eleven going on twelve and his handsome brother just three years older. All along Camden also ached, not from bad blood, nor the tragedy of a stricken youth, but from suffering the incontestable beauty, the utter beauty, of both his brother and the way he handled himself. To the end his brother remained relentlessly upbeat. Camden lavished him with readings of *Mad* magazine. He continually complimented Camden on his comic voices. Over a series of months, his brother's skin paled. He slid toward translucence, joked that he was turning into wax paper. It seemed less a joke to some, for indeed he had started to look susceptible to a breeze, to even a ray of sunshine. One afternoon he lost his power of speech, and the hospital initiated emergency procedures. During the night, he was moved into intensive care, where finally, after penning the nurse a note of profuse thanks, he slipped into unconsciousness and died. They were told that at his death he had no more substance to him than a glass of water.

Camden sighed. "I have to go back to the other room now."

"Yeah," said Eugenia. "Yeah well, I like boys, too."

"Fine."

"You're sure you have to leave tonight?"

"Why?"

"You could stay with me. I probably could use a little sleep."

"Yeah."

"Is that a yes?"

"I don't think so."

"Why?"

"I just, I'd feel, I'm not. . . ." Camden gave it some thought. "Well look, the whole band, all of us, we're driving to Baton Rouge tonight. There's no two ways about it."

"I won't bite."

Camden didn't say anything. The light-headedness had returned to overtake him.

Eugenia snuggled still nearer. "Don't you want to kiss me?"

Camden grew exasperated. "I can't!" He pushed himself up from the futon and left the room.

MEANWHILE, at Hickman's insistence, David'd urged, teased, nudged, and tickled Tanja inch by inch across the main room as far as the frontispiece of the hallway.

"Okay." Tanja had decided to share her screenplay idea with David. "Ready? Okay: a city called Regular, a character named Classic, and a lot of adjectives like industrial strength, family pack, that sort of thing."

David beamed. "That could be cool."

"Really?"

"Totally." David continued to work admirably to cajole her further into the hallway toward a bedroom. "I can see that."

Alas, at the frontispiece was where David's advance remained, halted at two in the morning as surely as if his shirtsleeve had gotten hung up on a nail. It was apparent (again at least to the bandmates) that Tanja had dug in her heels, that she wanted to stay near her friends, that she wanted to keep hanging out with the party and would surrender no more ground. David, to his credit, sensed this and nobly chose to retreat.

After Camden rejoined them, David spun to face the group. "Okay well, we gotta get going," he thundered while waving to all, and with that the band was finally rushing out the door, following his descent down the stairs to the driveway.

"Outta here," Pete Sosdring barked as he scurried out alongside Camden.

Only Eugenia followed them out. "Thank you for stopping by. We truly appreciated it."

They reached the minivan and Johnny was paraphrasing Martin Luther King Jr.: "Free at last, free at last, thank God almighty, we're free at last."

The doors of the minivan began to slam.

"Take care," said Johnny.

"Good-bye, Camden," said Eugenia.

"Baton Rouge," said Pete.

And away they drove.

THE four crossed into Louisiana sometime before dawn. Pete was doing the driving. He quietly played the radio. At a press conference in Riyadh an American brigadier general named Richard I. Neal was downplaying the accidental killing of refugees on the road to Amman. He emphasized little was occurring other than the continued softening of enemy positions, the hard bombing of convoy resupply lines, of fuel trucks. He refused to give out distances or targets, waved off questions regarding specific military hardware. Pressed on reports that missiles had been launched from subs, Neal could only say, "I cannot comment on submarines at all."

Pete suspected that, when Neal was young, bullies turned his name into a command: "Dick, kneel!"

Pete was tired, and wishing he'd gotten laid.

INSIDE Camden, strange yearnings remained unaddressed.

The sixth chapter, in which material is arranged, the Monkees and Hüsker Fag invoked, a long distance call placed, and lives arguably saved by rock and roll

THE MINIVAN WAS halted at a Baton Rouge intersection.

"This blows," said Pete, meaning the stoplight.

Lowery made exasperated sounds. "We've been sitting here for *hours*. It's like down here in the South, they're on a different kind of time."

Baton Rouge—the air thick with power lines, the honks of trains and riverboats, the rancid Mississippi smell, a service station.

"Rubber time," Pete agreed.

"Yeah, rubber time."

They were driving from the Riverland Suites Motel to the Chance Bar. It was afternoon. The boom box played an Ethiopian group they had all come to adore named Jil Jilala.

"Great groove," Sosdring groaned.

"Do you have anything to read?" Camden muttered. "My book's at the motel."

"Here." Someone threw him a crumbled-up souvenir program

of some sort. It hit him in the head. He began to leaf through it. It was entirely publicity pictures and fashion shots of three unattractive, apparently middle-aged men.

"What is this?"

"It's Hüsker Fag," Pete said.

"Hüsker Fag?" Camden asked. "Is that a book or a movie?"

"It's a band," David told him.

Camden's cheeks went red. "Hüsker Fag," he repeated.

"Hüsker Dü," Hickman clarified.

"It's a board game," said Lowery. "Swedish for 'Do You Remember?' "

"Oh," Camden replied. "Well, that's certainly very confusing."

The traffic light changed and the tape of Jil Jilala came to its end. Startled, Pete awoke to the minivan's gigantic disorder—filthy with chewing gum wrappers, hundreds and hundreds of matchbooks, shredded music magazines, promotional hats, maps used as Kleenex, lighters used as bottle openers, packs of tobacco and rolling paper, loose change, used-up cartons of Marlboros, a windshield ice scraper, smelly socks, dirty underwear—but most annoying, piles of loose cassettes all over, comedy tapes of truck-stop comedians, popular American music from the late sixties, the early seventies, the midseventies, &tc., &tc.—bolted upright, and screamed in terror, "Too many empty cassette cases now!"

SPRING was approaching. The sun already gave off some small warmth. The days were becoming noticeably longer. Early this morning the band had checked into the Riverland Suites Motel, which turned out to be a low colonial structure set in the swamps. They'd slept in late. Everyone was well-rested. Load-in occurred eight hours before doors opened. The club felt luxurious: two monitors up front, drum monitor in back, two monitor mixes. The space was nice; everything had a homey feel. The club owner knelt on the floor of the club, hand-stenciling Chance Bar T-shirts that he would later present to the band.

The only disagreeable aspect about Baton Rouge was that each night they were contractually bound to play either two sets or one extremely long show. David Lowery asked for a large piece of poster paper and a pen, listed out every song they knew. He added cover songs and a few numbers that he'd play solo. It still didn't seem like enough. This band hadn't been together that long. They barely knew the ones they played. "This is a challenge." Lowery sucked thoughtfully on the cap of a permanent marker.

Sosdring sought to convince him that they could yet learn more songs—there were many Lowery and Hickman half-wrote and left without finishing or arranging. Now they had the time, the setup, the focus. It should work.

Already, just ten or so shows into the tour, Sosdring dreaded a gig's redundancies like a dinosaur facing a tar pit. He was bothered by how Lowery talked obsessively about the past: "Once when I was a teenager," he'd say, or "I remember how, when I was with Camper"—talking as if he were seventy-five years old and doddering into extinction. THIS is NOW! So Pete—the agent of eternal change—pushed and pushed for new material, worried that otherwise he would begin to take too much for granted the precision of Johnny's solos (which never changed), the goofy stage antics (identical each time), the same set over and over, sometimes a bit dragging, sometimes a slight bit faster, but always word-for-word exactly alike, the same plugs for T-shirts, the same introduction of bandmates as "my homeboys," the same slouch with which Lowery leaned back and over and loosened his guitar after breaking yet another string (could he never buy a heavier gauge?), the same "improvisations" night after night; some nights the town was named first off and thanked, some nights perhaps the audience was more responsive, some nights the lights swiveled and flashed in dazzling color, some nights maybe the soundman didn't remember to snap off the overhead music until the band had begun, some nights T-shirts sold rapidly, the songs got shuffled into a new order, but without preventative measures, without precautions, eventually—Sosdring knew only too well—the routine of this job would numb them.

They hurriedly set up, dashed through an easy and reliable number—their old faithful, the three-chorder "Someday"—a small song, difficult to screw up, and one that they continued to open with nightly even though Lowery hadn't completed the words for the ends of most of his lines. To cover, he would scream a few nonsense syllables: "If you see a dark cloud—duw damnio! Don't be alarmed y gymraeg pedanddaithgah!" They got some levels on "Someday," then looked eagerly at Lowery. Without saying a word, he hit one chord, strum-strum-strum, hit another chord, strum-strum-strum, went on to a third, strum, then resolved it back at the first chord, strum-strum; the others soon grasped that they should join him in this—this was a song!

There was no one else in the bar at this hour but a man who sat on a stool with a heavenly yellow Miller before him. He was watching CNN, where eighty to ninety oil well fires burned out of control; there were aggressive reconnaissance and counter-reconnaissance border patrols and sporadic ground fire. The ground attack was expected soon. "If they want so bad to be martyrs," spoke one American G.I., "I'll do all I can to help." As the music started, the man withdrew from his coat pocket an inexpensive stopwatch with a long loop of string attached, wound it, let it run for sixty seconds, stopped it, reset it, moved to another bar stool, inquired of the club owner as to the price of his Miller, checked the stopwatch once more, paid, and left.

The problem was, Lowery hadn't prepared words for many of the newer songs. For example, he knew that in this song's chorus he'd talk about a tunnel, about how he could now see a light at the end of the tunnel, and how he hoped it wasn't a train. Pressed by the club owner to explain this lyric, Lowery contended it was a Dylan reference, though he didn't know why he thought that, or really what it referred to.

Sosdring immediately grasped the need for a gigantic chorus, to underscore the train, to emphasize the tunnel's light. Standing beside Hickman, Pete wailed a soulful harmony, and when Johnny dutifully copied the part, Sosdring climbed to the third in accompaniment. Sweet! With emphatic tosses of his head, he directed Camden on the requisite fills, on the duration of the appropriate cymbal splash.

They hit the chorus a bunch of times—it started sounding good—then worked on thoroughly dismantling the verse, which had to be parsed to its bare essentials to lend the chorus that much more grandeur.

It was a style of working, the rhythm section playing the groove over and over with whoever else happened to be around, grunting now and again "this won't work" or "yeah, that" or "one and, and, two and . . . and, that's right," formulating how they wanted it without any sort of top line at all, which musicians generally love but studio hands hate. It was the reason Glyn Jones stopped producing the Rolling Stones—as he'd once confessed to Pete in a limo ride to the Four Seasons. Jones found it too boring, sitting in the booth and just watching as everything was slowly leached of feel and excitement, played to death before the Stones ever got it put down on tape.

Using only grunts and facial expressions, Sosdring orchestrated a few measures of nice-sounding groove, carved it out successfully.

But something frustrated them; they all felt it. The song came to a halt. The bandmates studied one another, brains burning, faces blank, as they puzzled out the intangible musical ingredient that eluded them—tambourine? keyboards?

"I think," Sosdring reluctantly suggested, "we need words."

Lowery had nothing to offer, made no reply. He looked livid. He rolled a cigarette, lit it, called down to the club owner for encouragement. "How's it sounding out there?"

The club owner shrugged. "Quite cool," he said. "Very *Let It Bleed* with the ooh-oohs, the guitar evolving out of that very 'You Really Got a Hold on Me' Beatles-y riff."

Lowery stared.

Sosdring made loathsome gagging sounds.

"Still," the club owner went on, "I liked the first song a lot better."

"Well," Johnny smiled at him forgivingly. "But that was just a sound check song."

"Right! I loved it, very Creedence strummy Eagles 'Take It Easy'-like but with the guitar intro you totally stole from 'Lover's Rock' by the Clash."

"My good feeling about Baton Rouge," Johnny mumbled to Pete. "Poof!"

"Look," Sosdring barked at the club owner. "You gotta get off that side of the brain, man. Try listening with your dick."

They abandoned the tunnel song for a cigarette break, then gradually reconvened to try out another new number, a real fanny-twitcher. Again this one had no words, but Hickman had some ideas; he hauled out a notebook with a couple politely composed verses, passed it around, let them all partake.

Pete glanced through them—Aargh! All these super sad rock stars with their bad teen poetry, he thought. If they could advance past the idea of suicide as rude we might get someplace. This earnest pap was not what he wanted to hear anymore— enough! And Pete figured Hickman would know this as well as anyone . . . but no, there Johnny went, trying to convey something "deep" with these words he proposed, some "heavy" lyrics about the crazy Richmond characters he'd met.

"Not! Not!" Pete scoffed. "You're trying *too* hard. Look this has to be dumb. Dumb! Like, y'know, the *Monkees'* theme or something." A pal of his had done some sessions with Bobby Sherman—this was nineteen, nearly twenty years ago—a few of the sessions had been pressed on promotional flexidiscs and glued to cardboard as part of the packaging for Honeycombs and Sugar Pops. No overdwelling on sincerity there. People buying a grocery store product could cut along the dotted lines, play the backside of the box on their turntable, hear music. And that's all this business is—! pop heartthrobs, sugared cereal. Nothing more.

"Hey hey we're the Monkees," went Lowery.

"Yeah," said Pete, a bit agitated. "Like a song cheerleaders would do—but really over-the-top, way fucked-up cheerleaders. Like 'hey hey, it's okay' . . . um . . . 'mess your life up, man.' "

"Hey hey it's okay"—Lowery tweaked Sosdring's line just slightly—"to make a *little* mess out of your life."

"Cool," chimed in Johnny.

"There you go," went Pete.

"—uh excuse me. David?" Of course—with classic bad timing—it was the club owner. "Someone's . . . on the phone for you? Something . . . about an interview?"

Lowery looked significantly at his watch, mumbled expletives to himself and apologies to the others.

"Keep it short," Sosdring snapped as Lowery hopped down to take the call.

Camden sneezed.

"Hope you're not getting sick." Johnny sounded concerned.

He sneezed twice more.

"You get sick," Pete elaborated. "We'll kill you."

"—Never," they could hear David saying over the bar telephone. " 'Cause I'm there all along. I go along at the mixing sessions and I'm there when they master it so there's no way they can ever do anything to it. That's the best rule: Be there all the time. 'Cause then, if they want to fuck you over, they have to actually bad-vibe you, and nobody at a record company has a clue how to bad-vibe. I'm much better at it than they are."

Hopping down to go piss, Pete narrowly avoided landing on the T-shirts that the club owner had littered about the floor to dry.

"—went to Morocco," Lowery told his interviewer as Pete walked by. "I decided, 'Well, I want to do another band,' so I was trying to think of someone who would like the kinda music I'd been writing lately, I thought of Johnny, so I called him long-distance, and he joined me in Richmond. . . . We knew it would only be the four of us, and we'd be in the minivan and we wouldn't have a whole lot of big equipment or anything. And that we were just gonna have to do everything ourselves, no sound-man or anything. I mean, that's the way I used to do it with Camper all the time. I used to collect the money and just deal with everything and deal with any problems that came up, and I sort of forgot that it's actually really pretty easy. So I don't mind it. Even if sometimes it seems like we're on Boy Island or something."

Pete returned from the men's room, tuned up his bass, played some runs to keep himself loose.

"Baton Rouge," the club owner was explaining to Hickman, "it's like V.D., it gets your dick all spotty and red. The name comes from when whoring was legal down here, this was all whores in swamplands in the thirties."

"What heaven," the always horny Hickman whimpered.

"Yeah but lotsa V.D., you know, that's what I'm saying. Lotsa men with, you know"—he motioned melodramatically toward his abdomen—"baton rouge."

Lowery listened attentively to the interviewer's next question, like a diplomat receiving translations at the General Assembly. "My throat," he finally answered, "is just like covered in calluses by now, I've screamed it out so often, you know?"

Camden was draped atop his tom, his face resting on the head of the drum, either asleep or deceased.

"Hey," Sosdring spoke while absently fucking around with a bass riff from the Jil Jilala tape, bouncing through it with poppy quarter notes, then snapping and sliding it like Jaco on a fretless, constantly formulating, experimenting. "Hey, did you know that no two countries that both have a McDonald's have ever fought a war against each other?"

Hickman and the club owner looked dubious.

"Hey," barked Pete, "it's a fact, look it up, fuck off, &tc., thank you."

"—Frustration and the angry side of sexual yearning," Lowery was lecturing the interviewer, "rather than the resigned side of it. This conveyed musically, all done in a very profane way, in the sense of every day-ish. Not of the spirit, but in some way trying to find spirituality through all of that. That's what we're up to with this band, if you ask me. And that's not bullshit, the spiritual release of focusing on the profane."

"Christ," Johnny whispered to Pete. "This is ridiculous! This band never gets any girls. Blueballs tour, man."

"A no-wank tour," declared Pete.

"Make your own rules," Johnny said, running a hand through his perfect hair. "I had to wank in the bathroom of the club when we arrived the other night."

"Which one?" Pete wanted to know. "Which one?"

"Last night, I think."

Pete looked skeptical. "Houston wasn't a very good wanking bathroom. Big open room—HELLO!"

"Then it was the night before. Austin."

"You're incorrigible!"

"Don't encourage me, then."

"No, I mean." Pete rolled his eyes. "We can't take you anywhere."

"Is it my fault?" Johnny grinned at him with that annoying toothpaste advertisement of a smile. "I was dozing in the van as we drove up and I started dreaming and got this hard-on and had to run into the bathroom to wank. Blueballs tour, man."

Camden sneezed.

"You been tested for AIDS," verified Sosdring. "Right?"

Lowery laughed at something the interviewer was saying. "But the audiences are cool. For the most part, they're getting it. There's still a goodly amount of Orcas; oh, that's our name for them, the Camper fans, you know. They want to hear the old stuff. Right, it's inevitable. I know."

PETE grew impatient to arrange more material. Nonetheless, after David concluded the phone call he was needed for yet another interview, this one at the LSU radio station.

"You're joking." Pete was displeased. Their work had been going so well. "What about the music?"

"What about it?" David was putting away his guitars.

"When do we work on the music?"

David pulled on his jacket, his hat and gloves, looked at Pete. "Come with me. To the interview."

"No way."

"Way. It'll be exceptionally cool."

"Not interested."

"But I'm bored of hearing myself talk."

"So ask Johnny."

David did, Johnny agreed, and they went, with Pete reminding Johnny that David, naturally, needed guitar strings.

"I know," Hickman calmly said. "I was thinking of that."

The minivan drove off. The club owner left with them. He was needed to navigate. Camden and Pete were alone in the club. It was a pleasant enough place, a converted machine shop with faded Coca-Cola signage on the side, the walls covered with large paintings. Someone would come for them, a friend of the club owner. He would take them to the motel, where they'd hook up with Johnny and David. Later, they'd all head back to the club together.

Camden and Pete quit their instruments, went out front, and waited for the ride. Only in the South could they so casually leave their stuff behind in an unlocked club.

They each lit up a cigarette, looked out at the brick town, the red clay soil, the exceedingly green bushes. Crows screamed.

"I like this," went Pete.

A small corrugated-tin fort faced the parking lot from a field of clover and honeybees. There was a smell in the air that follows a fresh rain in the country.

"Yeah," Camden said. "Hey, you don't know, do you, whether Pensacola and Pepsi-Cola are related?"

"Huh?"

"You know. The city in Florida, Pensacola. And Pepsi—"

"Yeah, I heard you, I heard you."

"So, you don't know?"

"Who cares?!"

"Oh."

"I mean, God!" Pete shook a fist at him. "You gotta get off that side of the brain!"

"Okay."

The guy arrived after a time. He was pathetically dressed but his car was awesome, an old Fairlane in spotless condition. By then, the sky had drained itself of color and resembled a corpse. The day had turned so cold that what was coming out of the Fairlane's exhaust pipe appeared solid. The guy introduced himself—his name was Sammy—and then asked where they wanted to go for dinner.

"Dinner?" asked Pete. "What gives? You're driving us to the motel. The Riverland Suites."

"Oops, change of plans. Supposed to take you to dinner, actually."

Pete looked groundward and cursed. "Says who?"

"David Lowery. Talked to him at the radio station. Johnny and him are going to dinner with Henry."

"Henry?"

"Henry, yeah. Henry's my friend. He's the club owner. Think you met him."

"Oh," Pete remembered him now. "Well."

"So how about it? Where do you feel like going?"

"How about a place with a lotta eggs and starch?"

"Okay."

"He's joking," Camden pointed out.

"You're joking?" Sammy asked.

"I'm joking," Pete agreed. "Do they still make fruit? Everywhere we stop, all they got is eggs and starch. Like Denny's. 'Always Open.'"

"Always open," echoed Camden. "Like a shark."

Pete ignored him.

"They never sleep," Camden explained. "Sharks never sleep."

"Right, right, yeah." Pete intently looked away from him. "Don't you ever stop with that?"

They drove somewhere in, of course, no particular hurry. There was a lot of yielding, polite waving, wasting time at traffic lights. Pete was getting used to it though, no longer seemed to mind so much. At least Baton Rouge didn't pretend to be something it wasn't, like these places that look to be painstakingly reconstructed from photographs of Classic America®, faking homespun warmth with some dorky architecture and extra security. Baton Rouge seemed an ideal place to bash out music in tribute to one man's flagrant horniness.

"Is it always this cold?" Pete asked.

"This isn't cold," Sammy replied. "It's supposed to be winter."

"Oh yeah."

They passed fishing boats on sawhorses, tractors parked beneath overgrown bushes. The hood of the Fairlane shone. It reflected the other cars on the road. Pete watched the murky distortions slipping past. It was like seeing through soup. They came to a diner and pulled in.

It was your standard Naugahyde-and-linoleum place, with chrome-sided tables and chairs. They took a booth. The jukebox was playing a Lou Reed song called "Rock and Roll."

"What does this song mean, 'my life was saved by rock and roll'?" asked Sammy. "Literally? Like—"

"When was this written?" Pete interrupted.

"Late sixties. So maybe it was different then. Maybe rock and roll meant nothing but Phil Spector and Motown and Beach Boys, happy, blissed-out stuff. So maybe it was easy back then to know what this meant. It was a clear Us vs. Them sort of situation."

"Yeah," said Pete.

"Anybody who opposed rock and roll in those days was simply against kids being happy."

"Right." It didn't stay innocent for long. Pete was old enough, he could remember firsthand how complicated it all got. Distortion entered the guitar. Shows got violent. Words got mean. Things got real loud. Pete even felt partly to blame, he had a hand in this, all the posthippie seamy underbelly gloom with drugs and whatnot.

"But then," Sammy went on, "by the early seventies the legacy lost its bliss. It's hard to say now where an actual life could be actually saved by rock and roll."

Unless, Pete almost said, the noise itself brought you bliss, made you young and reckless again.

"I mean, 'My life was saved by rock and roll'? Like—"

"Consolation," Camden suddenly spoke up. "I think. Solace. Comfort. Consolation. That sort of thing. You know."

"As in, 'Hey I'm not the only fucked-up kid, listen to this guy, he's just as bad, so guess I won't gas myself to death in this stinky garage, here take back the keys, you can keep the car, I'm going inside to escape my ennui by listening to more of this here gloomy music'? You mean like that?"

"Yeah."

" 'Cause what I was gonna say," said Sammy, in the same breath, "was, I always get confused by that, how people always say, 'Hey this or that famous person saved my life.' Excuse me? Like Dylan always says Woody saved his life, that's one. And then Iggy says Lou Reed saved his life, Bowie says Iggy and Dylan saved his life, Morrissey says Bowie saved his life, and everybody nowadays, they love to say how, at some time or another, Morrissey saved their life. Such a fucking easy compliment. It always leaves me like all—hunh? These famous rock star guys, with their cold hearts and everything, wha'd they do, they reached in through the speaker and grabbed away the bottle of pills just in time, they snatched away the loaded pistol? They saved your life? Gimme a break."

"Yeah," went Pete.

The waitress swished up in her plastic dress. Sammy swatted her away. They weren't ready yet. They turned to the menus with halfhearted interest.

"Isn't there good barbecue around here?" Pete asked.

"Best soul food in the South, about ten miles off. Soul Shack. Rib meat just falls off the bone, very succulent. And a unique sauce, you never forget it, hot but sweet, just sweet enough, not too hot either, perfect. And the greens aren't bitter the way they often are other places, very fresh and cooked lightly, moist and crunchy. Lotsa homemade liquor there, too. And what else? Oh, the lemonade, hush puppies, corn on the cob. Wonderful!"

"Is it closed tonight?" Pete asked.

"What? No! The Soul Shack never closes, that's the cool thing about it. They gear up that wood fire to burn twenty-four hours a day. It's one of the secret ingredients. That's how they get the ribs so flavorful and delicate, their round-the-clock attention to the BBQ; lets everything cook slow and juicy. It's truly a marvel. Too bad we can't go there."

"Why not?"

"Oh, that's where Henry took David Lowery and Johnny."

"So? Let's go there."

"No, no." Sammy laughed. "I mean, you say that, but I know you don't mean it."

"Yeah I do. I want ribs. Soul Shack!"

Sammy showed his teeth, shook his head. "I've heard how it is. I've heard how on tour everybody looks forward to spending time apart 'cause it gets so claustrophobic always."

The waitress swished up again to detail the day's macaroni and cheese special.

Pete dropped his head into his hands. "Oh man."

They went around the table telling the waitress what they wanted.

Afterward, Pete questioned what Camden'd ordered. "What was that, an anus burger?"

"Angus."

"Okay. 'Cause I didn't see any anus burger."

"An Angus Burger. It was on the menu."

A new wave song titled "Love My Way" came on the jukebox. Sammy started speaking about the failure of every band to live up to its potential, how that made him personally feel like a failure. "Remember *Forever Now*?"

Pete and Camden didn't.

"Well, I was gonna say—okay, I was gonna say, well, if one album really truly saved my life, I guess it would be *Forever Now*."

Yep, thought Pete. I knew there'd be one.

"It's like, I can almost break into tears remembering how great Richard Butler was on some of those songs, so great that you could forgive their weak little disco songs, you could imagine a perfect album the next time they went into the studio. But whatever happened to the Psychedelic Furs? I feel responsible somehow, like I did something wrong, like it was me that went bad and not them. I mean, it was like they didn't get it, they didn't understand the cool things about themselves and after that album, pffffft, nothing. Took them three records to get that good, then they just flat out lost it, man."

"Huh," said Camden. He took a deep breath and released a tumble of words. "I guess I just listen to music differently or something, I can't hear what you're talking about."

"Well, be glad for that. It's a curse. It gets so you can feel it when someone's on the verge and it's terrifying."

This from a guy, thought Pete, whose life was only saved once by rock and roll.

"Nothing lingers like that promise, you get to be like an Ernie Banks fan, you don't want to hope 'cause deep inside you know you'll be disappointed, but you can't help but hope. Aztec Camera's another story like that."

The waitress brought iced tea for Pete and Camden and a milkshake for Sammy.

"Was Camper Van Beethoven like that?" Camden tore free a straw.

"Oh, definitely," Sammy answered. "But you see, they never made a bad record. They broke up before they got the chance. Each album was better than the previous one. . . . Yeah, they really terrified me. And probably, I don't know, some things they did comforted me that way you were talking about."

"They saved your life?"

"Saved my life. Yeah, maybe. I was just, there was this really tough breakup I had went through, I was eighteen. And just then that third Camper record came out."

"Sorry."

"No, no. I'm fine. It's funny. Most everyone shrugged off the breakup of Camper Van Beethoven, like how I shrugged off the breakup of, like, the Clash. At most they think of Camper Van Beethoven as the author of a few songs they liked. When they miss Camper Van Beethoven, they'll go back to their records, and play them, and be satisfied and think nothing more of it. I mean, I know, 'cause this is how the Clash works on me, I think about them, I miss them, I hear a song or two, it's put to rest, the end."

Their food arrived.

"Fuck!" Pete's grilled chicken salad was drenched in oil—not to mention his chicken was bland and watery.

"Did you ever see Camper perform?" asked Camden.

"Yeah," said Sammy. "Disappointing. They seemed bored. That's like a capital offense. There was this dramatic moment though, and it's one me and my friends still discuss, when every single band member stepped to the mike at the same time. I mean, each member had a mike. It happened only once that night—at the chorus of 'Take the Skinheads Bowling.' It just happened and, man, it was glorious. It was very Camper Van Beethoven; it had this feeling of total camaraderie, everyone side by side at the mike. It was also a moment that was very like the Clash, you know. Ironically enough. The group meaning more than the individual and all that. And it reminded me of what's important, to experience their songs live rather than hear them by myself, in my room."

They ate for a few minutes in silence.

"Hey, you guys do any Camper Van Beethoven songs?"

"Yeah." Pete was mopping his lettuce with a napkin. " 'Sweethearts.' 'Laundromat.' "

"Oh, 'Laundromat,' now that's one. God, I hate that song. I mean, I couldn't care less, I've heard all about how it's supposed to be a true story, and how the label insisted the song be released as a single and that Morgan had to be in the video, even though there wasn't any violin in that song, even though she hadn't actually played on any Camper Van Beethoven recording but was just accompanying them on the tour, still 'cause she was so pretty they were forced to put her in the video. But I just don't care, you know? All I hear, when the song is playing, is punk getting turned into nostalgia. Which is sickening. The last thing we were ever supposed to expect from punk was the luxury of nostalgia. That was the target of punk! Nostalgia requires a sense of self-importance. And self-importance makes music suck. But I know, I know. I'm bucking the trend, 'cause here it comes—punk nostalgia! The repackaging of old bands. The reunion tours. Guns 'n' Roses and Metallica saying how cool punk was. Gimme a break."

"I couldn't agree more," said Pete.

"They act like . . . it's weird, but people remember punk now like it was something that made money the first time around. Which it didn't."

"Right."

AFTER the awful meal Sammy interrogated Pete. He was surprised to discover how many things Pete had played on. They were heading back to the motel when Sammy asked if Pete'd ever met the Beatles.

"Nah." Pete looked off as he spoke, nearly humble. "Never met them. But I peed with Dylan once."

"Yeah? What was that like?"

Pete tried to recall. "Deafening."

"Yeah?"

"Yeah. Hadda lotta pee in him."

Sammy considered this. "I can see that, sure."

LATER, at the club, Pete unloaded it all on David.

"So you got lousy food," David shrugged. "And we lucked out. It's my fault? I asked you to come along, man. 'Not interested,' you said."

"Well, next time I'm coming with you."

"Fine."

"I mean it."

"Fine."

"There was oil in my shitty salad!"

"I heard you, yeah. As for our ribs, they were incredible."

Johnny inserted himself between them, urging Pete to take a stroll through the club and cool off.

This place no longer struck Pete as all that special. He tramped about, thinking how easily this could have been mistaken for the club they had just played, that identical feeling that what air remained had been wrung long ago of promise, like that in a hospital ward. Awaiting the show, people stood in clumps of three or four, some smoking, speaking little, rubbing at the ink phrases that had been stamped on their hands when they'd entered—pictures, words, library dates, &tc.—or tearing off corners of cocktail napkins and stuffing them in their ears. They looked, out of habit, at the empty stage, where there were only amplifiers and instruments in diffuse lighting—and where nothing stirred.

When Pete returned backstage David was reading a newspaper. "'You men of the air defense and falcons of the skies,'" Lowery declared suddenly, reading aloud from a recent radio broadcast of Saddam Hussein, "'consider from now on their damned imaginary lines north of the thirty-sixth parallel and south of the thirty-second parallel nonexistent. Surprises will be unleashed, and then it will be impossible to stop a new series of horrible surprises. O Muslims who believe in justice! Your faithful and courageous ground forces have moved to teach the aggressors the lessons they deserve! We have launched a lightning land attack, bearing high the banner, saying "God is great," and crushed the armies of atheism as they advance, routing those who could not run away while cursing the infidels and heathens!'"

"Double that," Pete murmured, "and that's how mad I feel."

THE gig went fine (anger helped). David gave Johnny twice as many bars to solo over, which fixed the dilemma of not having enough material to fill the contractual obligation. It wasn't the solution Pete favored, yet it worked fine. After the show, however, after the cords and the instruments were put away, there was just one chick still hanging around. Just one chick! And she had her eyes fixed on, of all things, Camden.

"Look at this," the girl spoke, opening her mouth to Camden. She had her tongue curled in a fantastic manner.

"What is it?" he asked.

"The Macintosh logo," she said.

"Yes. Yes it is."

"Only point-zero-zero-two-five percent of the population can form the Macintosh logo with their tongue," the girl informed him.

Camden idly responded with something about John Lennon that Pete didn't totally hear.

"Omigod!" The girl clapped her forehead. "Wait! YOU LIKE THE BEATLES?! Oh! My! God! I LIKE THE BEATLES! What are the chances of this happening, us finding each other?" She solemnly took Camden's hand. "Clearly this was meant to be."

Across the room Johnny jerked a thumb at the two of them, smiled. "Isn't that sweet?" he spoke proudly. "Camden made a special friend. About time."

"Fuck this," Pete said. He was both spent and fidgety, a frequent postgig phenomenon. His skin felt like waxed fruit that had been dipped in a bath of tar and nicotine, his mouth tasted of rocket fuel. His hair stank, his clothes stank, his head hurt. "I'm getting laid." He approached, keeping his gaze locked on the girl. She felt his stare, turned and faced him. She had light, shiny hair, ruddy cheeks, a button nose.

Pete leaned in front of Camden. "You know, the Beatles' first drummer was named Pete."

Her mouth tightened. "Oh?"

"Yep. How's it hangin'? Pete Sosdring. And you are . . . ?"

She frowned, started to laugh. "Oh my God, pee soft drink," she giggled. "Is that what you meant to say?"

"I said: Pete. Sosdring."

"Oh, sorry. Nice to meet you. I'm Marty. But I swore I heard 'pee soft drink.' Maybe it was 'peed soft drink.' The past tense."

"No," Camden said. "It was his name, Pete Sosdring."

"Forget about it, *Marty*." Pete's eyes narrowed. "Marty. Isn't that a boy's name?"

"*OKAY* now," Hickman stated accusingly. They were in the minivan—David, Johnny, and Pete—driving through pitch blackness to the Riverland Suites. "I will admit that this is the first time I have played this game, but still I gotta say, man: I think what you did definitely qualifies for a tonnage foul. Are there such things? Do we even allow for fouls? Because, if so, what you did there, trying to pry tonnage away from Camden. . . . — Camden! who has scored what, about eight points so far?"

"You're exaggerating," went Pete. "There's no eight-pound girls out there."

"That's your defense?"

Pete shrugged.

"I'm siding with Johnny," David announced. "How much should we fine you?"

Again Pete shrugged, and then did it a third time as well. He was good at it. "Forty points, see what I care."

"Forty? No way. More like a hundred."

"Whatever. A hundred then. Fine me five hundred. But you know what? I'll still kick all your asses. I are the champions, my friend."

David could scarcely deny this. "I just don't see how you do it either, with that smell you got. What is that?"

"What is what?" Pete threw David a good glare. "It's just the way I smell. The way I smell is the way I smell. More so after a gig." Johnny began to giggle, drawing Pete's ire. "At least I don't smell like you, Hickman. All soap and shampoo."

"Oh, that really hurts," laughed Johnny.

"God forbid," Lowery told Pete. "God forbid you shower now and then."

They started to sniff around Pete and guess his scent. David decided it was a little bit corn chips and a little bit crayons, but Johnny insisted there was the persistent odor of fried beef stirred in, too.

Pete lifted an arm and smelled himself. "It's the way I smell." He shrugged. "Processed cheese. What're you gonna do?"

"Could it be . . ." David mused. "Do you suppose it's some sort of aphrodisiac?"

"You look at his tonnage score," nodded Johnny, "And you think it could be. You definitely wonder."

Pete fell back in the passenger seat and closed his eyes.

ALTHOUGH the medicine cabinet at the Riverland Suites Motel said SUPPLIES INSIDE, it held no aspirin, no acetaminophen, no ibuprofen, and certainly nothing stronger. Instead, all Sosdring found inside were some wrapped plastic cups and a few discouraged slivers of puke-scented soap, neither of which would help to rid him of this atrocious Chance Bar headache.

He had his own room, for once, but the lodgings were spare, everything of quality stripped out, hauled away, as sharp objects are removed from a prison cell. Here he was again by himself, acute to that hour of early morning dead silence when every day things count off, get themselves noticed for a second, then abruptly reassert their place as ordinary objects. The nightstand popped loudly, the wall made a similar noise, a cooling tick, and other stuff followed. Through the pressboard ceilings came the details of his neighbor's actions—a shower curtain pulled back, the water pipes overhead shuddered in protest, a medicine cabinet squeaked open, shut. Pete heard his neighbor's television go on. It was muffled, an old man muttering in a fog.

Just two months previous, he'd been hearing these types of noises at his house, hearing in them the end of all his dreams, and now here he was. The sensorineural hearing loss seemed to be, as the doctor had said, nothing particularly important. But Pete missed his wife.

He pictured her then, the way she was, a sudden gust of happiness drifting through him. He nearly smiled. He saw her in a dark suit that made her skin pale, her brown eyes darken. It was a light, giddy feeling. His face tightened, cheeks dimpled. It was as if he were stoned. He remembered fucking his wife hard, this last time, and marveled that now he was masturbating to the memory, he had his dick in his hand and was thinking of his wife, and then with a rough motel hand towel he was wiping up semen, so much for a no-wank tour, and it was quaint, after all, how loyal he was to her, despite his slutting around. It tickled the cuckolds of his heart.

Afterward, Pete sought out a *TV Guide*. Late-night talk shows. But the *TV Guide* warned of inconvenient preemptions should the ground war finally begin.

He lay on the bed with the channel switcher and the telephone, dialing home.

"Hey," he said into the receiver, when the call went through.

"Hey," his wife replied sleepily.

Why was he calling? Now he couldn't remember. Hadn't he been missing her or something? It was tough to say. But he should give some reason, he realized. "Can't sleep," he put in simply.

"What time is it back there?"

"Late. I don't know."

He couldn't seem to stay interested in the telephone. A supermodel was confessing her unease to a much adored talk show host regarding the untold irradiating hazards of "stealth" technology and the biological counterweapons that no one had begun to suspect.

He grasped at something to say. "How's our little idiot?"

"Pete, now don't you call her that." His wife tried to sound stern but collapsed into laughter. "You know how she doesn't like that."

"Whatever."

"Yes, well. You missed her birthday."

"No I didn't."

"Oh no?"

"Well . . ." He waited for anything to come into his head, preferably something that might pass as humor. But now, with the orgasm past, he was too tired, sorta pissed off, couldn't concentrate. He couldn't even see the point anymore, really, of being funny. "Okay, I did. So?"

"Hey Pete, c'mon. Don't get that way with me."

"What way?"

"You missed your daughter's birthday."

"I—uh, okay. You're right. Happy now?"

"How about saying you're sorry?"

"Right. Okay."

"Jesus, who are you—Bad Dog Carl? I'm hanging up."

"Tell me what we gave her for her birthday."

"Barbies. Accessories."

"Malibu Barbie?"

"Malibu Barbie and her pals. Encino Barbie. Tijuana Barbie."

"What about Oxnard Barbie? I think she was at the show tonight."

"Her, too. And Barstow Barbie."

"Batteries sold separately."

"Yes, well. We stole the batteries out of one of the Casios you never use."

"All right. Fine. Did she at least appreciate the Barbies?"

"Good question! You wouldn't be the child's father by any chance now, would you? You're starting to sound like you care. I won't hang up. The answer is no. She only wants one thing for her birthday."

"Uh-oh."

"Guess what it is."

"She wants Daddy to come home."

"Huh? No, no! Nothing like that. Guess again. No wait, I'll tell you. What she wanted was to leave the door open."

"The door."

"The front door, wide open, every night: her one birthday desire. My nine-year-old daughter, all she wants for her birthday is that the house remain unlocked."

"Lemme guess. For the skunks."

"Seems somebody she trusts and loves very much told her that skunks live in the driveway or something but want to live in our house."

"Ah, little idiot."

"Who's the little idiot? Remind me now."

He could hear his speech slowing. He was falling asleep. "You don't suppose I could find a pet skunk for her down here in the South?"

"And drive with it the whole tour? Where are you anyway?"

"Baton Rouge."

"That's in Louisiana."

It took him a while. "You're right."

"So is that fun, Louisiana? Was tonight fun?"

"Oh. Another show, you know. Just . . ." He suddenly couldn't picture anything of the show except the encore. And he couldn't really tell her about how, when he came out in his underwear to play the last song of the night, a Cajun woman stood directly in front of him, pointing at his crotch and babbling in French to her date and—well, he couldn't help it—Pete started getting a boner. I'm fucking you all, he'd started thinking, smiling at the audience. I'm fucking you all.

"Honey?"

"It was okay. We have to keep grouping Johnny's mandolin songs together because it's the only instrument switch. It delays the set."

A yawn on her end. "The drummer any better?"

He didn't answer.

"Pete!"

"Huh? Oh, the drummer. Nah. So draggy, killing the tempo. When he's drumming . . . God, I feel like Jack LaLanne out there, towing a barge in my teeth."

"Where's Hanoi Jane now," the controversial guest host was asking a world-renowned television personality, "but in bed with this war's main profiteer?"

His wife yawned again. "*Pobrecito.* How 'bout this war, huh?"

"What war?"

"Pete. You're falling asleep."

"Yeah." He was going under. He struggled for words. "Guess so."

"Well, listen, I'm hanging up. But you know what?"

The phone was much too heavy to hold. It was impossible. It fell from his hand.

"Pete, you there?"

In the split instant before sleep he recognized his wife's voice, far-off and metallic, or thought he did.

"I miss you, darling."

HE awoke some time later. There was laughter on the television. A sharp voice on the telephone was prompting him to call the operator if he needed help. Pete fought to get the receiver into the cradle. After considerable effort he managed to do so, before passing out again.

The seventh chapter, in which a postcard is purchased, tonnage tallied, a producer offended, a secret gleaned, and a drunk tells war jokes

ONE MORNING SOON thereafter they were on their way somewhere, zooming past weedy fields and satellite dishes and prefab housing when, through a clump of pines, appeared a service station.

"All right," David grumbled. "Cigarette break."

Camden hopped out to use the rest room. Hickman trailed after him. "Last night was," Johnny said, "most fine indeed, most fine. Pete and I are getting this great thing of playing together, each of us has this certain kind of confidence thing. Like okay, I know how I relate to each one of these particular guys, and I know when he's slowing it down, I know when he's pushing a thing or there's a little bit of a feel thing, you know? Pete and I, we're sort of like . . . he's safety!—He's such a good player I don't have to worry about him at all—but he's not the lead singer. The lead singer is sorta steering the boat, so I gotta pay attention to him." They fetched the key from the attendant. Someone had crossed out the words "men" and "women" on the bathroom doors and substituted "pigs" and "angels." They went in. Camden took the urinal. Johnny continued past, locked himself in with the toilet. "Pete," he said, after positioning himself and sitting, "and I are getting to where we can do things together, we can hammer a groove down or we can let things start to fucking fray apart a little bit and it'll be okay."

Hickman fell silent and read the toilet paper dispenser. "Farting is such sweet sorrow," someone had written. He pulled a Sharpie from his jacket pocket and contributed, "Shock Orca." He giggled.

"What?" Camden asked, from outside the stall.

"Oh, it's just . . . Pete. Thinking about what he said. About the epic shit." Pete, who liked to label the different kinds of shitting, called an epic shit one where you felt your whole life proceed through you, like a historical survey, the complete inventory, things emerging that you would have sworn you never ate.

"God," went Camden, so faintly at first that Johnny wondered if he was merely talking to himself. "When I'm not up, I'm just not up. What can I do? And lately . . . When you're not up, what do you do?"

"You just do it." Johnny sat on the toilet snapping his fingers. "I mean, what choice do you have?"

"Yeah, I don't know." The urinal flushed. "Because I've felt kind of down. And dead."

"Well, even when I'm down and don't feel like playing I get up there and at least look and act like I love it. Plus playing with someone like Pete, he catches me overthinking all the time. He just goes, 'Ah, come on, man!' That's just being a professional in this. It'll come, don't worry. You're just beginning."

Camden had washed his hands. He hit the hand dryer. His

voice rose. "I think, I think around now I may need, I need reminding that I'm a good drummer. I keep feeling, always feel like I'm just, I'm under some real pressure. Do you know?"

"You were fine last night, man." Of course, he wouldn't mention that they had gotten the kid drunk, had made Camden down several successive glasses of Miller immediately before the set, but the experiment seemed to work, it caused Camden to leap ahead of the beat rather than settle back comfortably, and thence to catch up to the rest of them.

"Thanks," said Camden without conviction, and left. Johnny caught up with him again outside. He was studying souvenirs.

"Look at this," Johnny said. On the rack was a postcard of a key lime pie. On its back was a recipe. "I'm getting this for David. God, he'll love it!"

Key Lime Pie was the name of Camper Van Beethoven's last album. It was David's most thrilling work by far. Hickman had, once, amassed all the reasons why: because a pop album should, by definition, not be riddlesome; because it requires a gargantuan cadre of coconspirators to pull off such riddles with any depth, a harmonious crew of risk takers committed to making unintimidating challenges; because rarely do such albums succeed at seeming to be on the cusp of a new tongue, without precedent, raising the standard for how complicated pop songs can become, as hummable as they are meaningful; because there are very few popular recording artists whose employers give them license to be so brave; because—by 1989—nothing anymore beckoned both weird and friendly; because everybody, once famous, was appearing to don kid gloves, to spoon-feed their audience (or to become not even interested in maintaining an audience); and because too few were treating the listeners as intelligent and perceptive, as if lacking confidence that "they" would "get it"—despite mutual respect between artist and audience remaining one of the most beautiful relationships possible. Well, Johnny plainly adored *Key Lime Pie*.

Probably the success of it couldn't be credited solely to David. There was also Victor Krummenacher, the bassist. He'd played a major role. Johnny had known Victor for as long as he'd known David. Johnny had always liked him—Baby Victor. Perpetually six inches shorter and three years younger than everyone else. They met when Victor was fifteen years old, miserable one day, ecstatic the next, caught up in a scene of speed freaks, acid heads, and runaways, all gathered downtown in a great big shacked-up house. People were staggering into cars blind drunk and never making it back. There were hit-and-runs, overdoses, murders.

Hickman even bumped into Victor at a PiL show, the Olympic Auditorium, amongst a lot of violence, weirdness, 1981. The precipitously sloped floors—the only surviving major American arena built expressly for boxing—had everyone leaning into the stage. Punks balanced atop one another's shoulders to gingerly remove an antique clock mounted high on the wall. The Plugz opened, but they were perhaps unaware that knives had appeared, perhaps unsure—as Mick Jagger had been the previous decade—of the proper protocol when your audience members begin to stab one another. Hickman went down in the ceaseless heave of bodies, sure that he wouldn't come up; out of nowhere a beefy fellow bent and plucked him to his feet. Watching others go down and completely disappear from view, many at the front of the audi-

ence were grinning as they smoked cocaine. There were no security guards in sight, no emergency exits lit in red, no reassuring
voices over the intercom. A pall of mucous and spat beer hung
in the air like sour mist in a zoo exhibit.

"Cool!" someone in the middle yelled.

Onstage Tito Larrivo gamely continued to advance his Plugz
trio through all the tracks from L.A.'s first independent release
despite an avalanche of bottles tossed to slow his progress.

In the melee, a woman stuck her hands down Hickman's pants
and performed fellatio on him.

When Lydon emerged the frenzy increased. It was the first
time any Sex Pistol had appeared in Los Angeles. Everybody was
eager to make an impression. He promptly walked off, then
walked on again, back and forth the whole night. He'd sing a
fragment here, a fragment there, emerging from a hail of spit,
face coated in saliva; he'd sneer at the crowd and wander off.
Keith Levene, playing from behind his amplifier, also kept dis-
appearing; periodically he'd storm to the mike to tell the fans that
they were all so fucking stupid. Jah Wobble seemed consistently
there, he and a drummer, grooving on some low something or
another, awaiting accompaniment; but he too might very well
have been in and out, because everything about the night felt
murky and damp, except for the definite fact that people were
badly hurt, and the band furious, and the crowd thrilled. . . .

Well, times change. Hickman knew he was obligated to hate
Victor now, because from what he'd heard Victor was largely
responsible for engineering Camper's breakup, and Christ, that
had clearly devastated David. On the other hand, if not for

Camper's breakup, if not for David's summons from Morocco, where would Hickman be right now? Cutting hair for a living. Cutting hair and painting houses. Driving up to Bakersfield occasionally to play with any bar band that needed a guitarist, backing up a bunch of unknowns doing Louvin Brothers covers and standards like "Tennessee Waltz." So really he should be thanking Victor. Besides which, after all, there were Victor's *Key Lime Pie* contributions to consider. That's what it was all about, the making of great music.

But when Johnny somewhat ceremoniously presented the postcard of the key lime pie, David unexpectedly lashed out. "Gee, thanks, Johnny," he snarled, almost as if he were performing for someone. "I must have five hundred of these, I mean, everyone has been sending me these for years. . . ."

Johnny gaped in astonishment.

David looked knowingly at Pete, but evidently didn't get the laugh he was expecting.

In a voice intended to show he could stand up to such tough teasing, every bit as snotty and loud, Johnny retorted, "Well, fuck you then, man."

More embarrassed than anything else, David stormed off toward the bathroom.

"Fuck you!" Hickman shouted after him, and angrily folded a piece of chewing gum into his mouth. He passed the next few hours focused on that gum, chewing it far beyond any flavor. Its texture toughened, its color became that of putty. Outside the minivan, yet more weedy fields, &tc. Up front with Pete, David was vociferous about the sort of roadkill they'd just seen on Interstate 20, insisting it was a raccoon, an animal in defense of whose culinary reputation the great Johnny Paycheck had once murdered a man. Pete maintained it was a skunk.

"No way," said David.

"Look, who cares?"

"Well, I care, man. It was a raccoon. Besides which, skunks are cool. They get a bad rap but they're alright. They're furry, they're easy to house-train. They're an ideal house pet."

"Yeah yeah yeah." Pete bunched a windbreaker up against the passenger window, trying to sleep.

"We had some skunks hang around in Santa Cruz, they were friendly. And once, when I was with Camper—"

"Fuck!" Pete yelled.

Everybody froze.

"Not again with that Camper crap. Christ." He looked at David, settled back against his windbreaker. "Enough already."

Beseechingly, David sought Johnny's eyes in the rearview mirror. Johnny withheld his glance. For several minutes, David watched the road and said nothing.

"Johnny," he went at last. "Johnny man, I'm sorry, really."

He was ignored.

"Johnny, c'mon."

In the backseat, chewing his gum, Hickman grew fascinated by the livestock they passed.

"Really, I didn't mean to hurt your feelings Johnny. . . ."

For the next one hundred and sixty miles it stayed quiet, until Johnny rolled his window down and, finally, threw out the gum. "Guess it's time to total up some tonnage."

"Right," David agreed.

Camden raised a hand. "Put me down for zero," he volunteered.

"Yeah," said Hickman. "I didn't get any either."

David laughed. "Well, mine was Jewish."

"So?"

"I'm just . . . I think I deserve some extra tonnage points."

"How's that?" asked Johnny.

David was adamant. "You guys know what I'm talking about."

"Haven't a clue." Pete's tone was heartless.

"Mormons," said Johnny. "I think Mormons deserve extra tonnage points, okay. And possibly Druids. But a Jewish nymphomaniac? That's a redundancy."

"Maybe Jewish girls should count for half," proposed Pete.

Johnny nodded. "If that."

"No!" David nearly shrieked. "Come on. She was a hundred and seventeen but I deserve a hundred and fifty-five at least."

"A hundred and fifty-five gives you four hundred and eighty, which puts you in second place. Ahead of me." Johnny shook his head. "Forget it."

I might be getting some more action, Hickman wanted to add, if I didn't keep drawing producer duty.

Ten days into their tour, established producers had begun to turn up, sometimes as often as one per show, stopping by the motel to introduce themselves, coming backstage to offer encouragement before a show, showing up at their table during a meal. Others just appeared, casually, unannounced, as if they happened to be in the Deep South anyway, perhaps seeing the sights of Alabama. No matter, they always needed a host, and somehow it was always Johnny, it seemed, who got saddled with having to hang out with them every single time. They all possessed a striking look, a style, up to and including the calm fellow in the tailored suit and narrow necktie who smilingly observed their sound check last night and hardly commented; even he had a style, for he reminded them of George Martin and left them dreaming for a time how they could play off his conservatism with heretofore untold shenanigans, the playful yet brazen manner of early Beatles or early Clash.

"—Has it occurred to you," Johnny finally decided to say something, "that if I hadn't had to entertain goddamn imitation George Martin, then maybe I'd be on the scoreboard today?" Johnny took a breath. "Okay. And what about yours, Pete?"

Ah, yes, well. Pete had been spotted accompanying the tiny wonder in pigtails. Noticing her during the solo of "Mr. Wrong," Hickman had deemed the delectable treat too small and, like a fish, in his mind, he'd thrown her back. The name of the game was tonnage, after all. Yet the memory of her remained, the way she sucked on a Charms blow pop so hard it hollowed out her cheeks and widened her eyes, and how her pigtails flopped as she nimbly bopped to the beat of their rocking band.

Funny, Johnny thought. Here Camden is, the only truly single guy—David has a girlfriend, Pete has a wife and daughter, I have a son and a soon-to-be ex—and still, Camden is losing at tonnage. A score of 270 and, though Johnny would never tell, all of them pity points. It was all the way back a week ago at the Riverland Suites, exhausted after purportedly painting the town, that Camden last dragged a date back to the motel. It had never been Johnny's intent to eavesdrop on Camden's love life, but such things happened on tour with one's roommate, it just happened. In truth there had been very little to what he'd overheard. Some whispering. They'd cuddled. The girl, her name was Marty, had asked whether there was anything she could do to help. Johnny surmised there was some hardship in Camden's holding an erection. Johnny'd seen this Marty—she was plenty good-looking—so could only guess that there'd been too much liquor, for on occasion that would lead to impotence. It didn't seem to be bugging anybody too much, however; from the other bed, snoring soon ensued. So, that was that.

At breakfast the next morning Hickman had thought to nominate Camden for 140 tonnage points for his most excellent work with Marty. The others verified the weight estimate and offered congratulations. Camden didn't dispute any of the salacious details of the coupling fabricated by the others. He leaned his droopy chin on a palm and ate his breakfast. Johnny gave him a good-natured slap on the back. "Keeping his secrets," Johnny had spoken happily. "Like the cat that swallowed the canary."

THEY arrived at their next destination with Johnny still unable to forget Pete's special friend from the last gig. His head remained fixed on the pigtails and the blow pop. Hours later, after load-in at the club and check-in at the motel, Johnny fidgeted about the room he shared with Camden, inserting the pigtailed girl into various situations. He imagined her in *Hot Rod* magazine, in a black-and-white newspaper brassiere ad, on a Dallas Cowboy cheerleader calendar, amidst a cloying Victoria's Secret layout of supposed hesitance, of so-called Enlightened Shyness. He remembered the swimsuit issues sprinkling the bedroom with subscription cards, and realized it was already time to go wank in another video shop. He got a sudden idea.

"Hey," he told Camden, because Hickman's sudden idea was fiendishly simple: such a place will help awaken Camden's libido, will create the appetite where none now apparently exists, which possibly placed Johnny in the position of a pusher, that's unpleasant to consider, let's forget that came up. "Come on. We're going somewhere."

"Where?"

"Don't worry, don't worry. You'll dig it."

Johnny did possess an exceptional nose for such places and, despite being brand-new in town, a nearby adult entertainment outlet was soon located without difficulty. They entered to find the standard layout, the usual walls of sex toys and racks of paperbacks, the rhythm and blues playing overhead. Johnny acted as the tour guide. Over here are the shelves lined with erotic magazines; in the back are the dancers. They're never really worth the price, he explained, as they always keep you too busy reaching for your wallet and thereby prevent a decent, uninterrupted wank. Over there are the videos—organized as if by perverse census (age, race, creed, handicap, pain threshold)—he could especially recommend the anthologies of outtakes, the rejected bits in which the principals clearly had been deceived, had been assured this was for a lingerie shoot and not hard-core, or for whatever reason the crew could be heard mocking the action, the actress was in a foul mood, her bruises looked real. Seeing mistakes of this sort was a definite turn-on, sure.

Get change from the counter, he went on, feed it into those slots in the booths and switch channels till you find a video you like, see? And then you, as Pete calls it, let your jism speak. The beauty of this affair is that the semen can just be left on the floor. Guys with mops and buckets come by and clean it up afterward.

They both stepped to the register and each, in turn, asked the lovely cashier for five dollars' worth of quarters. She wore a simple pullover, a home-sewn affair that clung to her like Johnny wanted to, that erect carriage, squared shoulders, those wings on her back, ah, was that love, that crumble of collapsed sunglasses that hung from her neckline like he wanted to, the way her jaw angrily chomped her breath mint, the way she never turned her head when Johnny invited her to tonight's show, and counted to herself in whispers, giving him change, but hating him.

Johnny and Camden shut themselves up in separate booths, whereupon Hickman, fantasizing now about the cashier, inserted money, and eventually settled on a few slouching women in belly-button shirts with fingers raised, pale white bellies and pale blue jeans and uncertain expressions, smiles beginning to fade a moment too soon, a hint of suspicion registering in the eyes, a sizable amount of indecision obvious in their crookedly combed parts, chipping nails, heavenly thunder thighs, the beery beginnings of conscience ("Should I really be doing this?") in their sarcastically exaggerated Christina Applegate parodies. Signals from his brain traveled down his spinal cord to his genitals and sent blood flowing into his penis. His scrotum drew close to his body, his testes thickening. In the film naked models had sex while Johnny watched. He masturbated and tried, as he achieved orgasm, to pay attention to exactly what he was thinking. Was he imagining he was someone else? Or somewhere else? Was he imagining anything at all? He'd long been eager to know precisely how his brain performed as he came, certain that there'd be serenity in such a piece of knowledge.

But as always, he got blindsided by a loose fantasy, and failed to notice what occurred at ejaculation, and afterward, meeting Camden on the sidewalk out front, his penis was tucked away, forgotten and flaccid. His arousal level had plummeted to the point where he was now mostly full of sorrow, his sweet devotional one, his life's dependable love, but also preoccupied with how warm it was for this time of the year. What to make of these sixty-five degrees! Spring lurched at him like a hostile drunk, a vague, pressing annoyance. They were heading back to the motel. "That was pretty great," he said to Camden. "Huh?"

"Mmmmm."

Johnny gave it some thought. Standing in his booth, he'd been able to hear the audio from the channel playing in Camden's booth but realized he couldn't recognize it. "Did your booth have different selections than my booth?"

"I believe they were the same."

"Did you have, for example, on channel three, were there those girls doing things with long-necked beer bottles?"

"Yep."

"Okay." Then it dawned on him that Camden had been stuck on one of those channels in the middle, which Johnny always hurried past because they usually showed guys fucking guys— not his idea of a turn-on, nope, sorry.

But that explained a lot, Johnny admitted to himself, nonplussed and just generally unfreaked by the news—plus it also explained why Camden, man, was totally coming unglued. But what can I do, he wondered. Should I help in some way?

They came to a little market, went inside for some snacks. Johnny had a hankering for chips; Camden was expressing something about a Neapolitan ice cream sandwich. Oh, and while they were at it, they could stand to pick up bleach and laundry soap; none of them had done their clothes in some time, at least since Texas, and the minivan now smelled of a locker room. They selected their items, waited in line, paid for them, immediately opened the food packages, were walking again; the whole time, Johnny was hitting his head, trying to recall the right words to say to Camden. What is the language of comfort? It was on the tip of his tongue.

Later, in the laundromat, as they made decisions about mixing colors and whites and about what fabrics required warm water, the dryers pounding and clunking behind them, and then drifted from reading evangelical interpretations of the gulf war in the local paper to watching, in a sort of reverie, their suds swirl, Johnny felt himself nagged by a need to speak up. But with what? All he could think to do was to advise Camden on how to improve his tonnage scores—for example, you might ransack your brain for former lovers who moved away and might be nearby now. This, though, presupposed previous relationships where none might exist, judging by Camden's lack of braggartry of a sexual past. Better than that he'd advise something less obnoxious, like that Camden call on relatives who live around here and urge that they introduce him to available dates.

Then, too, given his age, how much could Camden accept

about himself? So he liked to watch guys fuck guys, did that make him gay? How much was he ready to admit? Johnny knew what it was like to be bugged by the truth. For example—this was the instance he always thought of—he knew a woman who had her automobile painted in a very experimental pattern, a bash of colors. It looked as if it'd been bombarded by paint balloons from a rooftop. And once she complained to Johnny that when she drove around, for whatever reason, male drivers honked at her and grinned. They yelled for her telephone number and worked to articulate, in the few seconds they had while halted alongside her at a red light, of an profound longing to pleasure her carnally. This happened on any given day regardless of her particular appearance. It was as if by simply driving a car this colorful, she beamed mating signals, waved the colored feathers of a seductress. Johnny sympathized with her complaint, although later—and this was where it got sticky—he admitted to himself that he would've done the same: the honking, the grinning, the yelling, were he to come upon such a colorful vehicle. And in truth he may very well have done exactly that, once or twice, without realizing that was his friend in the driver's seat. This bugged him, just as it bugged him to acknowledge that he, too, without ever thinking about it, liked to look at big-breasted women. Was it ugly but true, perhaps, that men judged a woman's sexual mores by the size of her breasts? If so, how unfortunate. A woman really had very little choice about her breasts, you know (short of plastic surgery).

As for Camden's condition, Johnny still didn't know what to say, but later, in the back of a bar, the band was felt-penning mean-spirited sarcasm on the already oversketched dressing room walls—remarks that insulted their record label, their manager, their audience—basically anybody whom the band owed a debt of gratitude—"It has to look," Lowery chortled, "like we're feuding with everyone"—and they even wrote graffiti ridiculing Lowery's former bandmates, their preference for wicker-encased amplifiers, which David felt looked like lawn furniture—as they chatted with a producer who had flown out expressly to probe their willingness to work with him—a sloppy-shirted fellow with a mess of uncombed hair, too small jeans, beat-up deck shoes—a much-lauded hipster bringing breakthrough popularity to a few obscure groups who could barely play, could barely sing, who constructed "atmospheres" and referred to their songs as "compositions" and "themes"—when the producer, taking a look around, suggested this band should be named "Vendetta"—and in response Lowery grew very calm. He strolled to the window, set a hand on the pane to gauge the outside temperature. He opened it to the breeze. He would get someone, he insisted, to write a piece called "We're a Bad Trip," which would tell the ASTONISHING but TRUE story of his last band's breakup.

"Number one was that Victor, what we did is . . . during January Camper did some rehearsals and during this time Victor was really freaking out 'cause he'd broken up with his girlfriend of two years. Well, he told everybody else in the band why he was freaking out and why he broke up with her and stuff, well, not everybody, but Victor was going through a lot of personal things, he started doing a lot of drugs and stuff, and it was because, as I found out six months later, I found out, it was because he'd come out of the closet. And decided he was gay."

Pete snickered. He was across the room doing breathing exercises, stretching, loosening up his voice. He sang some scales, swigged some Miller, puffed a cigarette, sang more scales. Camden spilled tobacco everywhere. This was common, for he always struggled in hand-rolling cigarettes. He kept filling the paper too full, maybe failing to support it adequately or moistening the lip too much, doing everything wrong. Hickman went over to help. He required a flat surface and so used the top of the condom dispenser, where Pete had just written, "Don't chew this gum, it tastes like rubber," to go with what he'd previously written at the bottom of the urinal, "Don't eat this cake, it tastes like soap," which, truth be told, was considerably funnier than the matched pair written there before, "Nothing is in the intellect which has not been previously in the senses—Saint Thomas Aquinas" above, in another hand, "Nothing is in the toilet which was not previously in your mouth—So do this: Please flush us." The problem with those last two, as Hickman saw it, was that the final one was too over-the-top, way too gross (and the soundalike of "Aquinas" and "Please flush us" was much too strained), which overshadowed the otherwise ingenious (you had to admit) parallel of things in our senses leading to things in our brains while things in our mouth led to things in the toilet. Brilliant, that was, but so badly put forth in this instance as to be unappreciated. Johnny completed work on Camden's cigarette and handed it over to him.

David went on. "The first time I heard it was from somebody I didn't even know, who just heard that that's what had happened to the band. He came out of the closet; it's a very important thing, actually. And actually, you know what? I always knew Victor was at least bisexual. There were a lot of things that . . . a lot of people have bisexual tendencies. But this was different. He decided to come out and tell people about this. Except me. Which is strange. I had known him longer than anyone else in the band."

The producer poked at a hole in his Levi's, made no reply. Pete angrily took up a Sharpie, started to scrawl a joke that belittled Victor Krummenacher for being gay, but Johnny intervened and crossed it out. The producer explained that he was really more interested in hearing the perspectives this particular band had on, for example, let's call it, selling out.

"All these people," Lowery complained. "They talk about selling out, they just don't get it, it's like you might consciously write something trying to be merch—like the Pixies. Black Francis always sounds totally uncommercial to me, but then when I heard 'Digging for Fire' I was, like, oh, this is Black Francis trying to write something merch. I mean, you can hear that."

"What is it," Hickman suddenly asked, "people think there's some elite group, some pie in the sky, and everyone has sold out to join—"

"Look, it's like," said the producer. "Everybody wants to be heard but if your music is about being alienated, an outcast, then how many get to experience it? If you sell, like, two million copies, get nominated for Grammies and all kinds of acceptance, and the majority embraces your alienation, is it at all honest to portray yourself as a rebel?"

"Yeah," said Hickman.

"Like, did you see that thing about how the Persian Gulf special forces, this past week, they've been barraging the populace of Basra with noise to disorient them, playing Missing Foundation from helicopter gunship loudspeakers and, like, GG Allin from their offshore gunboats? I mean, a month ago, this music meant rebellion. But now that it's a government weapon, who knows what it means anymore."

"Does," Lowery had to know, "the Pentagon pay ASCAP any fees for these songs, broadcasting, performance royalties, that sort of thing? God! The right band could really clean up in a situation like that!"

The producer ignored him. "The only real question is, can you keep the mainstream's expectations out of your mind during the recording process? I think selling out is, people trust there are things you might not do to get popular, things that are beneath you, and when it turns out you try these things, people call that selling out."

"Yeah," said Johnny. "I call that making a living."

"So is there anything you would NOT do to get popular?" the producer asked.

"Nope," Johnny answered quickly. He felt like telling this guy to piss off; apparently that's what would be required if Hickman was to ever score any more tonnage. "Nothing. We'll do whatever we have to do to get David's songs, and my songs, heard by the most people possible."

Well, that did it. From that point forward, things didn't go so well with that producer. By showtime, he'd departed. Johnny was free to study the audience, to dream of finding a date down there, to watch the women's underwear—now *that* was something over which a woman has a choice, what sort of underwear to put on, and almost certainly it said something about what they were expecting from their evening. If she was in pants, what was her ass saying, was there the wide cotton outline, the narrow satin, the thong, or was there no panty line, and therefore, quite likely, no panties at all? Did her brassiere clasp in front, was it a push-up, a backless, a low-cut, underwire affair, adjustable satin straps and triangle cups, or beneath that stretch lace chemise was she just brazenly braless?

Sometime, it must've been during the bridge of "Central Valley Mud," Hickman caught sight of a blonde in a mesmerizing bustier, her cups lightly padded, the hook-and-eye closure in back. She smiled at the attention and, after the show, came up to the stage and introduced herself. Her name was Sally. Johnny invited her backstage. On the way he slipped his arm about her waist. Again she smiled.

Backstage Camden was oiling his high-hat. David was french-kissing a woman. When he saw who it was, Johnny nearly flipped—he's always so lucky! David's special friend was the lovely cashier from the video store! She had unexpectedly taken Hickman up on his invitation and come to the show, the one with the home-sewn pullover affair, erect carriage, squared shoulders, sunglasses, breath mint. Immediately, Johnny regretted choosing this blonde with the bustier. He wondered how bad it would look to demand that he and David be permitted to trade.

"I," said Camden, "still say Negative Cutter." Ostensibly, there was a conversation going on back here, again talk about what to name the band. "You remember. The credit from that awful Justine Bateman movie we saw in Baton Rouge."

Sally moved across the room, called over the cashier, whose name, it turned out, was Linda. They both saw Pete's graffiti on the condom machine and started giggling.

"I just want some meaningless name, a one-word name," said David. "Some meaningless, one-word band name that everyone can overanalyze and read a shitload into—like Cup. I mean, we went through Cup, they already ran it for a conflicts check back at Virgin, it didn't work out. Now I have another, they're checking out that one."

"What is it?" Linda asked David. She and Sally had helped themselves to some Millers.

"You know I can't divulge that." He shrugged his shoulders. "Ah, what the hell. It's Flower."

"Flower," went Sally. She chugged down her entire Miller and went for seconds. "How sweet."

"Is that F-L-O-U-R," Linda asked, "or F-L-O-W-E-R?"

"Flower," David said. "Though Flour is kinda cool, too, now that you mention it."

Camden examined them sadly with faded eyes and slipped away.

"Hey, is he okay?" Sally asked. She was on maybe her third beer already, or her fifth. They were like candy to her. "I mean, your drummer guy just took off like . . . is something wrong? I was always told drummer guys are maniacs but that has to be the quietest little drummer guy ever."

Johnny wanted to make the excuse, but David spoke up first. "There are actually two kinds of drummers, you know," he said simply.

Sally nodded. "Oh, right."

Meanwhile, Linda was making a thoughtful face. "Anyway," she said to David, "going back to that, since you asked. Yes, I am an artist. In fact, right now I'm writing a novel about women who dance naked for men in booths and how their attempts to talk are endlessly frustrated."

Johnny rolled his eyes at his date. Sally stared back woozily, licking her lips.

Lowery was intimidated by Linda. "Wow."

Sally initiated a drinking game called Area Codes (player gives challenge of an area code's three digits, other players must either identify the area code's geography or swig the sum of the area code's numbers) and within fifteen minutes the case of Miller was empty.

"Can I ask you a question?" Sally said.

David nodded.

"How do you get your face to sound that way?"

"My face," said David. "My face. Do you mean my voice?"

"Oops." Sally giggled. "Yes."

"My throat is just like covered in calluses by now, I've screamed it out so often, you know?"

"Oh yeah," went Linda. "I read you saying that in an interview once."

They climbed into Sally's car, some American sedan, and drove to a bowling alley that she knew. It was open twenty-four hours. In the corner, large men sat on stools, still as boulders, pouring alcohol into their bodies. Paint peeled off the ceiling in Doritos-size chips. The place struck Hickman bleakly.

"It was awful a year ago," Sally suddenly spoke up.

"What was awful a year ago?"

"Everything."

It was that vague. Johnny put his arm around her and didn't question her further.

They took a table in the bar and continued drinking Millers. The bowling alley featured live music. It was one guy doing songs from the seventies. It made David and Johnny very happy to drink while hearing this stuff—the most natural, the materials readily at hand, the glorious stadium dudes of their youth, the sexy, the strong—and they started to tick off the forgotten greats, "your Judas Priest, you got your Steve Millers and Pat Travers types of fellows, your masterful Blue Oyster Cult, your long-haired trippy soul of a growling guy, Leon Russell!"

The musician announced an intermission, placed his plastic piano upside down in his lap, and began shoving replacement D-size batteries into its opened back. "That's where we're headed," Johnny heard Sally say, and thought: Oh no, not this again. He knew this stale diatribe: The robots are coming! And they're bringing dance tracks! Synthesizers in the seventies were supposed to replace rock bands. Drum machines in the eighties, they said, were going to make drummers obsolete, and electronic samples would be tomorrow's melodies. But—ha! and ha again!— electronics would never replace the rock band, which remained man's greatest invention.

The barmaid visited them often with tray after tray of drinks and munchies. Sally launched into telling jokes. "How do you break up an Iraqi bingo game?"

"I don't know," Johnny winced.

"Call B-52."

Johnny looked stricken. Linda and David made like this wasn't happening. Was this woman telling war jokes? They adopted a selective deafness.

She was undaunted. "How many Iraqis does it take to screw in a lightbulb? Well, it doesn't matter. There's no electricity."

"That's okay," David said. "You don't need to tell jokes. We're really not in the mood."

"Wait. One more."

"You sure got a lot of these," said Linda.

"What's Saddam's favorite video?"

"Um. I give up."

"*Honey I Scud the Yids*. Oh, wait! I have a camera! Let's everybody take pictures."

"Let's everybody not," went David.

"Oh, come on, please, it'll be fun," said Sally. She thrust the camera at Linda. "At least take a picture of me with my studly little guitar god here."

Linda grabbed it. "Fine."

Sally batted her lashes at Linda. "Please?"

"I just said I would!"

Being next to these breasts no longer meant a thing to Johnny but embarrassment. He was bored even with her bustier. He slouched, roughly corralled Sally in a so-called affectionate head-lock, stuck his paunch out. The camera focused in. Sally grinned, struggling to balance herself against Hickman so as to not tumble straight into his lap, both hands steadying on his leg.

The camera's flash drew the attention of a man in a yellow hat across the room, who now made eye contact with Sally. A sort of vulgar consideration flashed across his face. Johnny became uneasy, at first worried about getting in the middle of some brawling action. Then he was overcome with bliss, imagining that someone might actually step over to relieve him of this nuisance. Sally put the camera away in her purse and the girls together went to the bathroom. Johnny grabbed at David across the table. "Okay, I have to ask you a couple questions now and it's not just because I'm really drunk; or yeah, I'm lying, it could be, really drunk. But quickly now. Where are we, who are these ladies, and what's going on? Five seconds for each query. Now go!"

"Are you kidding?"

"Only about the part about what's going on. I'm really fucking inebriated, my David friend. Does mine have a name, I forget."

"Oh man, I've long since given up on solving that one. Really, what is going on? You're not actually going to sleep with that woman, are you? I never thought I'd ever ever ever be saying this to you Johnny, but—you're too good for her."

"Yeah, how about that!" Johnny laughed. "Do I score extra tonnage since mine's a moron?"

"Only if I do, since mine's in Mensa."

"Oh, I got it—Linda, that's her name."

"No that's mine. Yours is Sarah."

"No it's Serry! Jelly! . . . —Sally! That's it!"

"Are we in Jacksonville Beach?"

"Are you serious? You're wasted, too! Jacksonville Beach was days ago. No, we're . . . somewhere else."

"Okay, then yeah, Sally, that's her name, sure."

"We played a show tonight, right? What do you suppose happened to everything? I'm thinking Pete and Camden took care of the equipment."

"I'm thinking that, too, yeah, I hope. I know Pete has the motel keys and the key to the minivan."

"Fine, I'll stop worrying."

"You do that."

The girls returned, and everybody waved at the barmaid for another round. The musician had long since finished for the night.

"Sometimes we're all, I'm thinking, we're like doing this tour and eluding the radar, we're furtive," Lowery said. "They'll look back later in history and wonder how we slipped through and, like, managed to stay out of sight, while being this cool. Then, I'm like—"

"Hello?" jeered Linda. "This is your brain. Can we talk?"

"—Yeah. On the other hand, I'm like: Nobody knows. And, nobody the fuck even cares."

"There you go." Linda gave him a pat on the back.

David lit up a cigarette and they passed it around, as if it were something illegal rather than tobacco. "God. I wish we were in England now. We'd have a single out by now."

"Get over it," Linda said, with some smoke in her lungs suddenly sounding a frightening amount like Pete. "You're very much not in England."

David couldn't stop. "And then, I don't get it. Wouldn't you want to know why Camper broke up? Why aren't more people asking me this? I'd be so like all, 'Hmmm. You must tell me everything!'"

"So you do think people remember you?"

"Well, I mean. Shouldn't they? Unless the world is . . . I mean, I fuckin' don't understand this shit. Check my pupils, am I stoned?"

"Hmmm. Well, you're drunk. No question there."

"As are we all," said Johnny thickly.

"Everybody's drunk!" the blonde in the bustier cried, flinging a basket of pretzels into the air. "Hallelujah!"

David watched the pretzels approach the filthy ceiling and then head back down. They hit the floor in a million pieces. He reached into his back pocket, unfolded something. "Look." He smoothed the creases out against their table. "Look everybody what my good buddy here bought me."

"What is it?" asked the blonde.

"It's a postcard!" David grasped Johnny's shoulder in fervent gratitude.

"Nice," said Linda.

"It's a key lime pie!"

"Right."

"Isn't it wonderful? I mean, this guy is so great. He's my best friend!"

Johnny beamed at David.

"Everybody," David yelled, "my best friend here, Johnny Hickman!"

"Johnny," the blonde formally shook his hand. "How do you do?"

He turned to his date in bafflement. "And you are . . . ?" Johnny asked.

The man in the yellow hat continued to watch them. David burrowed close to the cashier, as Johnny wished he could. "Tell me about this book you're writing," David said to her.

"It's called *When the Hundredth Coin Drops*. It's really about the whole, you know, effects of porno."

"What's a hundred-coindrop?" asked David.

"A hundred coins! Don't you know? At those video arcades they only allow you to insert up to a hundred coins."

"Video arcades? Why?"

"Because they're worried what'll happen."

"When?"

"When the hundredth coin drops! Duh, hello? Oh my God— am I here all alone?"

"Is this true?" David asked Johnny, who nodded to verify this woman's facts. "And why wasn't I keep abreast of such developments?"

Johnny looked apologetic. "Sorry, sir." He winked at Linda.

"You know what I do?" his date wailed. "I have a government job! Don't you want to know what I do?"

Hickman scarcely responded. "Okay."

"I'm the hygienist at Fort Jackson."

"I take it back, I don't want to know."

She longed in the worst way to be a mysterious member of the entourage, never identified yet enigmatically affiliated, but she lacked any of the qualities that that role requires. If we get her somehow headed in the opposite direction, Johnny was thinking, then we can ditch her. Or maybe we encourage her to go meet this man in the yellow hat. He was still staring at them, closely, a regular Curious George.

"That's a very big job," his date went on. "Do you realize the horror of conditions at Fort Jackson? I'm not alone, of course, but there's no one helping me, I might as well be alone, the way I'm always out sweeping that darned parking garage, it's so terrible! And now that's all I can think about."

"I'm sorry," Linda said. "I lost you. What's there to think about?"

"Oh." Johnny's date sighed. "Nothing. I guess."

Across the room the man in the yellow hat was standing now, with his coat on, and throwing money at the table. Now he was laughing with the bartender and broadly sweeping his arms, and heading outside, and starting up his blue convertible, and driving away. Johnny looked glumly at the table. No one, it seemed, would rescue him from this woman, whose name he'd once more forgotten. She reminded him of something he'd heard once, that when a girl starts to become annoying, it is sometimes hard for a guy to figure out whether he should say aloud how much he hates her or—instead—just have sex with her.

"I want you to leave," he spoke right into her face.

"You are too cute, you know that?" She let out a low snicker, which grew into a giggle and continued for some time. "I'll leave but only if you *come*," she leered.

"Do you realize how easy it would be to kill you?"

Again she laughed.

"No kidding. People disappear all day long, nobody knows where to, they're just gone. Dead, probably."

"It's true," David corroborated this. "Johnny's in tight with the police in California. He knows these things."

"How thrilling!" Sally's eyes glinted.

"With a sharp enough knife I could cut off your hands and your head and your feet and leave your torso to be found at the quarry and they'd never figure out where you went. You know that?"

"Oh, you're rich!"

"I'm Rich?"

"Like they say," Sally responded gaily. " 'Watch out the cruel but more / Beware the gentle, who will hurt the worst of all.' "

"I'm curious," Linda asked. "Afterward, how would you dispose of her feet and head and hands?"

"Dissolve the flesh in a chemical compound. Put the bones in a Tupperware vat weighted with quick-dry cement and heave it in the swamp. Voila!"

Sally cackled, thoroughly enjoying herself.

Linda applauded Johnny's plan and then squeezed David's arm. "Let's go home now," she purred. "I'd like to fuck. I'm calling a taxi." She left, returned, snatched David, blew Hickman a wet kiss, and departed. The waitress came over to sweep up the shattered pretzels. She also swept up the key lime pie postcard, which had fallen to the floor some time ago. She carried it away in her dustpan.

"I hate my life," Johnny told his awful date.

"Naturally," she smiled.

The eighth chapter, in which a
shipwreck upon Girl Island is
pondered, bad interviews granted, a
future in garbage glimpsed, and an
opening act restores lost faith

THEY WAITED IN the faculty lounge for the opening act to
end. They were to play the student union. They sat very still in
hard plastic chairs pulled close to the cafeteria tables. They
smoked, and tried not to think about what they were hearing. It
was another vile band, this time an all-female vocal combo
called Sweet Singers of the Heart. They had landed nothing but
shitty openers this whole tour. All to David were clear examples
of the timidity of today's music, but none more so than these
touchy-feely girls whom Pete called "Sweet Suckers of My
Farts."

What made it worse was that these same Sweet Singers had
already opened for them twice before (they, too, saw a lot of
Highway 10 this month). Some tour manager must have worked
hard to synchronize the two tours, believing they'd make a fantastic double bill, the gentle women paving the way for the ruth-
less rockers.

David and Pete had conversed with the Sweet Singers the

second time, in Tallahassee, why not, they had contraltos in the band, which meant tonnage. It hadn't gone especially well. The Sweet Singers were also baffled about why their bands had been booked to play together so much.

"No offense," spoke one with curly black hair. "It's just that the goddess energies we tap into onstage don't seem to inspire you."

"All Charlayne means," apologized another, "is that we play women's music. While you . . ."

"Yeah." David saw their point. "And we play men's music."

"That's very well put, yes!"

Leaving Tallahassee, Pete pronounced the Sweet Singers to be lesbos. He even floated a new name: "Sweet Lickers of the Clit." David, however, was more used to feminists. He disputed the dyke vibe that Pete picked up.

"I bet," went Johnny, "they hate always having to open for rock bands. You know? That'd probably be a drag, as tiring and smelly as a tour is. They arrive at the next gig and oh no, there's more boys with more loud guitars."

"Playing their men's music," Pete agreed, "to a roomful of men."

"Right."

"Man." David was doubtful. "I don't think they're all so dainty, just 'cause they're chicks, I just don't think so. I bet they're sick of each other, sitting in their van going, 'God, let me out, let me out! What am I, on Girl Island or something?!' "

"Oh!" Hickman's face shone. "I would very much like to visit Girl Island!"

"I know, I know. Maybe we'll shipwreck there one day, 'kay?"

· · ·

AFTERNOON gigs were always draining, and the gig at the student union this afternoon turned out to be no different. In this sense David was greatly relieved to take the stage after the wussiness of the Sweet Singers. The contrast alone ensured that their set would rock plenty. Still, who likes dancing in daylight? The audience hung back, and in that way, playing to a room filled with stiff, overeducated spectators, it totally felt like a Camper gig, so much so that it sorta creeped him out.

"You people," David said around the middle of the set, once he noticed all the pensive looks. "C'mon, now. You're thinking too much, we can pick up on it." He chose one girl in the crowd, a gorgeous, green-eyed goth with purple lips, crucifix earrings. "C'mon. Get off that side of the brain." She had dark hair, the full-length outfit. "Come over *here*." He beckoned. "It's *warm* over here." She screwed up her eyes, smirked, stuck out her tongue. David had to laugh. They ripped into the next song so loud, whatever it was, it tore through like a demolition, it made his sleeves rattle, his pants cuffs vibrate around his ankles. David was happy. He leaned toward his guitarist, screamed. "Johnny!" Johnny couldn't make him out. "Johnny, man! I want to fuck your hair, Johnny!"

Johnny nodded pleasantly. Later, at load-out, while a Baptist sorority gathered on a nearby lawn to celebrate the sanctity of life, Johnny wanted to know what that had all been about.

"Oh, I just," David seemed a little embarrassed, "I'm just totally totally happy, hey I look over and see my good buddy here on guitar and he looks a stone cold fox with his such excellent hair, shiny in the light and shit, totally excellent, the length and shit, hey I just couldn't help it."

"Yeah? Couldn't help what?"

"I wanted to fuck your hair. So I started screaming about it, 'Johnny, I want to fuck your hair, I want to fuck your hair, man!'"

"Oh. Okay."

"You couldn't hear me?"

"Not really, no."

"It was just the moment and everything, man."

"No, no. That's fine."

"Besides, I'm not the only one who feels that way. I bet," David looked around, seeking a target for the joke. He saw the sorority girls—no, they wouldn't work—then Camden walked through, dragging the trunk they called the death case. "I bet Camden does! Don't you?"

Ignoring him, Camden continued off.

"Don't," went Hickman.

David got defensive. "What?"

"Don't bad-vibe him like that."

"I wasn't bad-vibing him, man."

"Just don't."

"Why?"

"'Cause I say so."

"Oh yeah?"

"Yeah."

"You know what, Johnny?" David was deflated. "That thing I screamed at you—about wanting to fuck your hair—it's just not there anymore, man."

"I'm very sorry."

"It's okay," David sighed. "It was bound not to work."

Maybe Johnny was an emotional genius, but it wasn't as if David didn't have eyes in his head. He could observe Camden having a bad time with the band, the tour, evidently uncomfortable with the fit. You didn't need to be a rocket brain to see that. It was apparent just from how Camden jammed his hands in his pockets (so hard that his pants sagged), from how he drooped along (like some winter tree over the water).

Lowery felt for Camden. Hey man, he understood. But what could he do? Fortunately or not, David had gone to school with a lot of people who preferred never to spare feelings. He got mocked a lot, mostly for pronouncing words wrong, eventually got pretty thick-skinned. Even so, and granting that, he could still, when necessary, draw upon plenty of hurt lingering from those days. He'd probably been a loser (plenty of times still feared he was). There were his beloved folk and country records that he remembered playing only when no one was over, for he was scared stiff that his friends would laugh if they knew. Lowery happened to adore that old-time stuff, but it was terribly uncool, the music of a time capsule, nothing new or flashy, one ancient microphone set in the middle of a rod and peg, pine-floored cabin, the singers shouting through the decades to be heard, the sound brittle and dry.

In high school Lowery would try to tan alongside chicks in bikinis—"laying out" they called it—but always managed to say the wrong thing, either too direct or too brainy or not smooth or droll enough. Ah man, it was terrible. What do you say, what do you say? This was the quandary of his youth, the hormones, mouth drying in fright, the sight of a bikini turning him to

160   *Camden Joy*

Jell-O. That had been a really bad time. Even now, almost two decades later, Lowery often had to tell himself no, he wasn't a loser (he probably used to be, but he wasn't anymore). Sure, he knew how Camden was feeling.

AN Orca from the student union wanted an interview for the school paper. David told the band to finish load-out and then wait for him. David followed the Orca back around to the faculty lounge, took a seat among the remnants of their deli tray, chewed on a carrot. Just over the Orca's shoulder were broad double-paned windows through which he could observe Johnny, Pete, and Camden in the parking lot.

The Orca asked first how their tour was going, any evident features of success come to mind? Lowery responded with atti-tude, a strong, direct confidence, sensing all the while he wasn't conveying the desired impression. The Orca would prefer that David confess to missing Camper. But he couldn't do that, mainly because it wasn't true, nor could he be grumpy about how rough touring was, though it was fashionable just then in inter-views to whine how we're wasting our lives out here for you people, we wait five hours, we do three hours of sound check, we wait four more hours, we play you an hour of music, don't we have it just awful?

Avoiding that tack David instead segued into his favorite theme, inquiring as to the fate of dangerous white music. To where had it disappeared? Everyone lately was making academic distinctions. They were so serious, pompous, preachy, holy. Granted, it made sense not to treat this music as purely a stupid, childish business; it's important to be efficient, to make a living, it's smart to set up a reliable income, to worry about whether you'll have enough money when you're sixty-five. Nonetheless, everybody, all the press and the bands, everyone just has to loosen up a bunch. It's about danciness, audiences have to be treated as equals. Most musical complexities exist out of insecurity, for the sake of showing off the songwriter's smarts.

The Orca translated Lowery's words to mean the paradigm of indie music had become exhausted and by 1991 was meaningless. He perceived Lowery's new group to be the introduction of a new paradigm, a cunning send-up of a southern rock band. Lowery's defense, his excuses for this style of boozy music, must be intended as expert irony. That can't possibly be what he means! For a time, the journalist went along with it all. He had every intention of giving Lowery's act a chance. He nodded as Lowery advocated furthering the "mongrelization of rock" by drawing on the "glorious stadium dudes" who, Lowery insisted, made people really wanna get down, which was an important role nobody fulfilled these days. The Orca found these concepts remarkably sinister, but he nodded anyway. He even agreed good-naturedly that ZZ Top and Aerosmith were better than any eighties band! Ultimately though, he balked.

"Aw, come on," the Orca said softly, rapping the table. He couldn't keep pretending. "You and I both know, that stuff sucks. ZZ Top? I mean, what you're giving me, this is like a parody of an interview, right?"

Lowery hadn't expected this. He became tongue-tied, wondering if he had talked to this Orca before; well, if not him specifically, then at least to his breed. He knew these Orcas only valued bands that were secrets, bands nobody heard, bought, or talked about. *What a phony criterion.* What these Orcas wanted Lowery to be went against common sense—he should elude fame? One lousy publicist is all that requires—one lousy publicist and some bad distribution. If that's all it took to be credible, why should anybody sweat the songwriting? Orcas like this held that only by leading a depressed, impoverished life could one summon up "integrity," whatever that was.

"How can you legitimately play country music?"

"What?" David wasn't even pissed so much as bored.

"Well, you have to admit you're faking it, right? I mean, you're from the suburbs." The reporter even had someone in mind—he didn't share it but he was thinking about it—a character named Adam Cramer from a novel by Charles Beaumont, the writer of all the best *Twilight Zones*, those ones where everything's a dream and everybody's got amnesia, only the greatest television programs ever!—in this novel, Adam Cramer arrives in the South, an outsider, fomenting racial bigotry solely to prove the fundamental correctness of a philosophy known as nihilism. Wasn't this what Lowery, too, was doing, as someone who'd graduated from the University of California with honors in math after solving an allegedly impossible calculus problem, pretending now to be ignorant, a regular cowboy from Hollywood, talking with the bad syntax of a Southerner and singing classic rock out of the worst sort of cynicism and greed?

Now Lowery was pissed. What did that mean, he fumed, what did this Orca just mean, 'to play music inauthentically, as imperialists rather than simpaticos'? People had some pretty fucked-up ideas about what made certain music cool to listen to and play. "Man, you know, there's nothing pure about any of it, nothing authentic anywhere. You know that, right? Music isn't better when it's played by poor people. It's better when it's played by creative people."

"Okay. Sure, David."

"I'm serious."

"Right. Whatever you say."

David was preparing to punch the Orca right in his little smartass smirk when, looking out the window, he saw Johnny bet Pete that he wouldn't streak the Baptist gathering. He saw Pete nonchalantly discard his clothes and go prancing out of sight. Momentarily, David saw Baptist sorority girls race past, clawing at their eyes as if to scrape clean the memory of what they'd just witnessed. David chuckled at Pete. Johnny was cool, Johnny was his friend from way back, but still Johnny was a Catholic boy at heart, with a guilty conscience and a crippling sense of fair play—now Pete, there was somebody plugged into the world in the right way.

"How about you tell me why Camper broke up?"

"God." David had been waiting for this. "That's like all you people want to know, where Camper went! I don't want to have to keep being asked about Camper for the rest of my fucking life. But okay, you want to know, you really want to know, you want to know why your *precious Camper* broke up, I'll tell you why."

"Thank you."

"—I'm in all kinds of turmoil, getting pretty psychotic from all the touring. And I'd been going out with this woman for six years and I'd left to record *Key Lime Pie* and when I came back home from that she had like found somebody else. And then through the first part of the *Key Lime Pie* tour—you see, we started in July and went all the way through to Christmas, and in this time I like broke up with this girl and got back together several times and stuff like that. It came to a head. I probably shouldn't even be telling you this. But I totally wigged out, tried to kill myself in Denver."

David pointed at his wrist. "I cut my veins here. Almost immediately, as soon as I did it, I realized . . . it hurt. I decided it was a bad idea. The sheer pain set me off or something. So I was bleeding and pretty wigged but it was sort of cathartic. The next night we did one more show. But I'd lost a fair amount of blood and I wasn't feeling well. I never told anyone in the band. We canceled the last three shows around Thanksgiving. Salt Lake City, Idaho, and, I think, the university in Eastern Oregon. We took ten days off.

"So then I went and I took my tour money and I flew to Richmond, where I'd met this girl on Halloween and had been corresponding with her and calling her a bit and stuff and called her up and said, 'Look I'm really sick and really fucked-up. I need to get away. I don't want to go back to California. I don't want to deal with any of this. Can I come stay at your house? I'll tell you what happened when I get there and stuff.' And I stayed at her house for a week.

"And this is my current girlfriend (we started in a very bizarre way).

"Anyways, so I was not really mentally stable over the next few months. . . . God, I can't be telling you this. Enough already."

The Orca smiled happily. "Yeah, sure. Thanks, David."

"God!"

The Orca reached to shake David's hand. But David wouldn't touch him, and left the faculty lounge without saying anything more.

OUT at the minivan Pete had gathered up his winnings and redressed himself. David climbed in. They drove to the motel. Johnny was sorting Mass Murderer trading cards into his lap, in stacks of those still unsolved and those wrongly accused, while complaining about the proliferation of prowar slogans. They seemed to be frost-painted on virtually every window in America. The band gave this some thought. It used to be that they felt okay about the war, it was sort of like a private joke or something, but that was when they were back in the land of liberals. Now, in the gung-ho Christian South, Hickman suggested putting ABANDON OUR TROOPS in big letters on the side of the minivan. That, or maybe: SUPPORT OUR GAY TROOPS IN THE GULF.

"That's another thing war's good for," announced Pete, his thoughts apparently elsewhere. "Inventions. Better inventing goes on in wartime."

No one replied.

He was right, of course.

DAVID stewed about the interview in the faculty lounge, but as it turned out, it didn't compare to Charlotte. In Charlotte, the next day, the truly unbelievable came to pass. David spoke the words "Camper Van Beethoven" in an interview, and nothing happened.

"Who?" The interviewer didn't know David Lowery had been in another band before this.

David's jaw dropped. He had to stop the interview, he couldn't continue. Camper had been broken up less than a year and people apparently couldn't wait to forget them, to wipe them off the radar, to clear that shelf space for a billion other "interesting" bands. He was distraught that all his past work should be so handily dismissed—but then why be so surprised? It's a very hard thing getting remembered. There's a resistance that has to be overcome. Nothing lingers, he reminded himself, everything sweeps past. Take, for example, this war. If you shut your eyes long enough, the war would go away. Eventually people would dispute it ever happened. Whatever the war accomplished, whatever it achieved, would be forgotten. And if they're okay with forgetting a whole war, then by all means they'll discard popular entertainers in a heartbeat.

Talk about your irony, thought David. Now *that* was ironic. The lifespan of the culture shortening even as the lifespan of its members was lengthening (an inverse relationship, that was called). Which means—he had to address the cold, hard facts— that soon very few people are going to be able to fund any sort of retirement at all from the writing and recording of rock music.

And where would I go? David wondered. What would I do?

He imagined himself at work in an office building, like before, when he worked at the paper during summer break—the building lit at night with the softest Miller yellow, the cubicles with their snapshots of felines or infants (or a couple exasperated comic strips), the unanswered phones ringing above thick, off-white carpeting, all of it awash in the gentle roar of fluorescence, thrumming with electricity, as telex machines spat news from across the globe.

Or there was always bike messenger. You didn't make a lot of money, of course, but he'd met plenty of cool folks who had that occupation. It put you in shape, racing to get your packages crosstown, swerving in and out of traffic. David always considered it vaguely romantic—the urgency, the subculture, the outdoors. Even the way you'd see them pedaling bicycles with their lockup chains over one shoulder and across the torso, even that was kinda cool, although it made David think of slaves in shackles. Still, that was cool, because in truth they all were slaves, you couldn't escape that, that's the way this crazy world worked, so why not just pedal harder and wear your goddamn chains and proclaim it.

But in truth David knew where he'd eventually end up, because his last girlfriend once had read him his future from a cup of tea leaves, and it had been most vivid and convincing—he'd work at the waste management facility, the end of the line—nothing soft, nothing tolerable, no escape possible—and everywhere he looked, all day long: trash, trash, trash, trash, trash. The routine was simple. Earthmovers'd open gashes, dump trucks'd deposit trash bags, tractors'd cover them. This would occur sometime distant, after his career's leap to sudden stardom and inexplicable crash-and-burn, with his multiple divorces and twenty-first century days of opium but a memory. David would be old and waiting to die. He would drive a water hauler, the sprinkler truck, softening the ground for the others. A fecal pall would fog the area with a nutty aroma. He saw himself wearing a mask over his mouth and nose. He was holding a cap gun to scare off the gulls. It was not a life he especially looked forward to.

Over the telephone at the Charlotte club that evening their A&R man Mark read David the credentials of interested producers. All the names of the acts and the titles of their recordings reminded David of the mountain of garbage he'd plow in his old age. David spoke into the phone all the reasons these producers wouldn't work, citing various noteworthy shortcomings, but mostly he remained thinking about the city dump, feeling afraid. Did it have to be so, he should've asked his girlfriend after the tea reading, wasn't there any way to appeal this fate? "We have to make this like Madonna," David suddenly told Mark, the solution having come to him. "You know?"

"Madonna? Oh, Madonna Ciccone, of course. For a moment there I didn't know who you meant. Ha ha ha, that's a joke."

"I'm laughing."

"Madonna. Okay, no, I don't know what you mean. You mean, a million-seller with a thousand ancillary tie-ins? An immense publishing income? A label of your own, maybe a film company?"

"Yeah, like that. Financial security."

"That's fine with me, too, David. Just for the record, we're in complete agreement on that. I'll just make a note here to be sure and inform each and every producer that they will only be considered if they also want to be incredibly successful. I imagine it'll really narrow the list, though, huh?"

"Your sarcasm is duly appreciated."

"Okay, I'm writing this instruction to each producer, 'Make this like Madonna.' Okay, done."

"Madonna with an edge."

"Oh, with an edge, sure. Like Terence Trent D'Arby? Isn't he Madonna with an edge?"

"Yeah—but, okay then. Terence Trent D'Arby with an edge."

"Oh yeah, I'm on top of that all right, no problem."

"Again, fucking sarcasm."

"Well, you know enough about what you want, you guys should just produce it yourselves." It was an end-game remark, something Mark liked to suggest because, as he and David both knew, it meant tremendous savings on the company's investment when a band did this.

David's response was to strike the receiver against the wall. He kept at it for a time. "Mark?" he said once he stopped. "Mark, you there?" He banged it a few more times. "I think the connection's getting bad, can you hear me?"

Mark was laughing. That was a good sign. It meant he got the reference, he'd seen *Pee Wee's Big Adventure*. Virgin Records was okay, man.

They spoke a bit more. When he hung up, Johnny said, "Hey, you never got strings today, did you?"

Lowery cursed. "Man! I should have made one of you guys do it."

"I cain't think of nuttin' I'd ruther do, Massah Lowery."

"God. Everyone's sarcastic tonight."

For once—thank you very much, Mr. Booking Agent!—that night's opening band wasn't the Sweet Singers. It was a trio of boys playing appropriately loud rock music. After the trio sound-checked, David sought out the frontmen. They were in the club's antechamber, working the pinball machine. Both seemed about twenty, dark hair cut collar-length like the 1966 Rolling Stones.

One was so absorbed in a game as to be virtually indisposed. It was a spectator sport, watching him. He played each ball for at least ten minutes. Secret stashes of points were continually being uncovered inside darkened housings or plain-seeming corners of the pinball machine. His use of the side-flippers was additionally skillful, averting the "tilt" shut-down such an aggressive style would've earned a less sure player.

David said hello to the guy who wasn't playing, who looked tidier, better shaved, hair combed, had his shirt tucked into his pants.

"Oh, hi! Wow, David Lowery!" The guy beamed. "How do you do? I'm Jeff." He extended a hand, indicated the pinball player. "That's Jay."

By way of greeting, David praised his high score. Jay turned, in a bad mood. He glanced nearsightedly at David through his bangs, then snapped another ball into play.

Their immediate differences of personality gave Lowery the gut impression that this band, these two, would split up, maybe quite soon. Maybe they'd just fought, in fact. The fissures were too visible. Jeff was every bit as outgoing and pleasant as Jay was shy and morose. No matter how much brilliance Jeff gave off, Jay's presence soaked it up, so that standing beside one another they struck a nearly invisible balance.

"Hey man," David now recalled. "You guys were supposed to open for us some other time, weren't you?"

Jeff shrugged. "Yeah, sorry about that."

David gestured in reassurance. "No prob." Jeff'll grow up to be chubby and happy, David predicted to himself. He'll wear a tie with a button-down shirt, maybe suspenders, work in retail. On the other hand, this Jay guy, he's already a lost cause. Too slim for construction work. Looks like a trash man. He'll probably be in the earthmover while I'm on the water hauler, now wouldn't that would be something well worth anticipating. "I heard one of you got ill or something?"

"Nah." Jeff laughed kindly. "Well, our van—"

Jay interrupted with something inaudible.

Jeff added volume, repeated it. "Van-itis, yeah. Vanitis. Our van got sick."

Last week, come to think of it, someone was telling David about these guys, calling them the new Meat Puppets. Lowery could recall only a few facts. They were three kids from outside St. Louis. They had a cassette. It was called *No Depression*, the name of a Carter Family song. Now that was a promising reference! The Carter Family were one of those uncool, old-time acts Lowery had long ago been forced to keep secret from his school friends and enjoy in shamefaced privacy. —Cool!

Jeff asked if they could request a song, which put David in mind of why he'd come talk with them in the first place.

"For a set of strings," went David, "absolutely."

Jeff responded with a merry guffaw.

David was serious. "That's what it'll cost you—oh, plus a Camper T-shirt. How 'bout that? A set of strings for a Camper T-shirt and we promise to play your request."

"You don't have strings?"

"Couldn't get to the store and . . . I need some, in the unlikely event that, y'know, I break one tonight."

"I see. Extra light or light?"

"Light gauge."

"Darco Funkies okay?"

"Fine."

Jeff looked toward Jay for approval. Jay shrugged without turning around.

"Yeah, okay." Jeff crossed to their pile of equipment, pried free Jay's case, counted through the packaged strings to guarantee a full set.

David remained standing behind Jay at the pinball machine. Jay was frozen, looking down at the machine. He had his hands on the flippers but no ball in play.

"Go on," urged David. "Keep playing. I'm liking watching." Momentarily, David heard him mumble a response about "no quarters." David fished around in his own pocket, came up with some change, enthusiastically slapped it down on the glass. "Here, go wild." It wasn't much, a few dimes and nickels, some pennies, two quarters. Without a word Jay put the quarters in the machine and pressed reset for another game. He pocketed the rest of Lowery's coins.

"There we are," Jeff was back, pushing a set of strings into Lowery's side.

David nodded his thanks. "It's really a bargain," David tried to justify himself, "with the shirt thrown in."

"Yeah, well," said Jeff. "We'll give you a shirt of ours too, how about?" He had retrieved one while getting the strings.

"All right."

He handed David the shirt. David shook it out, took a look. A black T-shirt with simple yellow lettering—nothing on it but their band name and the name of their hometown, Belleville, Illinois. David doubted he'd ever wear it, but he pretended to be impressed.

"Now then," David asked, "what's your request?"

"It's a Camper Van Beethoven song."

"Yeah. But we're not great with . . . yeah. Don't know if we'll be able to but, yeah. Our drummer's kinda, y'know. But what song?"

" 'Sweethearts.' "

"Yeah, that's a good one. We maybe could pull that off. God, 'Sweethearts.' I remember, we wanted it to be the single but Virgin overruled us, made us put out fucking 'Matchstick Men' instead."

"That must've gotten tiresome to play 'Matchstick Men.' "

Just then, Pete happened by. David informed him of the exchange that'd been tendered.

" 'Sweethearts'?" Pete asked, glancing at Jeff and Jay. "We already play that every night anyways."

"Shhhh," David waved his hands. Embarrassed, he turned to Jeff, started to apologize.

"Keep the strings," Jeff smiled. "Don't worry about it! We just want to hear 'Sweethearts.' "

"Cool, cool. Thanks. And tonight," David pointed at Pete, "I'll have you know, we're featuring a bassist named Pete Sosdring."

Jay perked up. "Piece of String?"

"No," Pete looked at him crossly. "I'm afraid not."

"That's right!" Jeff was delighted. "Hee-hee. 'I'm a frayed knot.' Very good, Piece of String."

"Pete," Pete said. "Sosdring. Not Piece of String, whoever that is."

"You any relation to that piece of shit we got on drums?"

Pete clenched a fist. "I am not."

David couldn't tell if Pete was honestly mad. He held back his laughter, not wanting to piss Pete off further.

"You're a knot?" Jeff blurted.

Jay's smile was there but hardly detectable. "Could Piece of String be feeding us a line?" he said, suddenly audible.

"Man, you're terrible," Pete threw up his hands. "Just, shut up and go die."

Jay shrugged. "Fine."

"But first," said Jeff. "Tell us a ripping yarn, would you?"

"Fuck—!" Pete backed away. "Whyn't you just—go fly a kite!" He bolted backstage.

"Go fly a kite, hmmm." Jeff gazed thoughtfully at Jay. "That also qualifies as a piece of string joke, yes, okay."

David chuckled. "Okay, I should go back and make sure his feelings aren't hurt beyond repair."

"The poor dear."

"Thanks for the strings, man, and maybe I'll talk to y'all later."

"Well, don't forget to get us a T-shirt."

"Oh, right! Yeah, don't let me manage to forget that. Please. After the show or something, 'kay?"

"Okay," went Jeff.

.   .   .

DAVID'S sense from before, that this band was about to break up, could not have been more wrong. Watching their set, he suddenly understood. Yes, they were diametrical opposites—Jay hiding behind a harmonica rack and never speaking between songs, Jeff bouncing about the stage, chatting everybody up. But this was the drama of their sound, in a way; Jeff's fat bass notes in support of Jay's intense, erratic guitar. They played like boys who knew each other completely, a sloppiness expertly reigned, sudden lurches executed perfectly, like the Minutemen (another tight trio, led by two guys who'd spent their childhoods dashing together through sprinklers, tempting fates). Both Jeff and Jay sang. When Jay sang alone it was almost unbearably moving (Jeff's voice was not so breathtaking). They particularly sang well together, neither voice on top, a complementary blend.

David was utterly charmed, and even contemplated putting on their T-shirt. It was really a pretty cool T-shirt, come to think of it. David considered Jeff's demeanor. They have that generosity, he decided, of a desperate band just beginning. It reminded David of when Camper was just starting out, they had the first record out and toured the southwest with the toxic inks and the xylene sloshing around the VW squareback, and they silk-screened shirts in the parking lot and sold them for six dollars apiece, which almost paid for gas, and they had zero cash after the trip and decided to quit until the highly successful R.E.M., having heard their record, telephoned out of the blue and invited them to fill the opening slot in a leg of their ongoing tour, which rescued them, gave them confidence, recognition, and money. Well, David thought, it's possible that before these guys lose their spark R.E.M. might save them, too. They were still performing charitable acts.

David grabbed Pete as he walked by. "Tonight," David first thumped him in the chest, then pointed deliriously at the opening band, "the shitty opener is blowing us away, man!"

Pete narrowed his eyes in disagreement. "We'll see about that," he said, like a gunslinger challenged to a duel. "We'll just see about that, won't we?"

*The ninth chapter, in which the
ground war at last starts and Camden
awakes in a panic of sadness*

WITHOUT WARNING, A journalist for some local weekly
demanded access to the whole band. David paced about a motel
room and prepped Camden what to say, what not to say. Don't
use any real names if the tonnage contest comes up. Tell him
the per diem is generous because well, I mean, it is. Describe
the music's subjects as i) the angry side of sexual yearning,
ii) the spiritual release of focusing on the profane, and/or iii)
frustration. Got that? If the journalist starts a string of associa-
tions, just nod your head. Journalists like to treat music as if it's
intruding upon a very private dialogue they've been having with
a few lucky know-it-alls. Who understands what the fuck they're
even saying?

But when Camden finally got his chance, with the Walkman
on the coffee table documenting his every word, he was mostly
asked about himself. This turned out to be astonishingly easy,
the simplest test he'd ever taken. He discovered the answers to
these questions were there all along, filed away inside him. He'd
just open his mouth and there the answer'd be, having been
pulled from the stacks and immediately dispatched by some ter-

ribly undervalued employee, ready for delivery. He talked about drumming with a lot of party bands in Richmond and then, as the journalist fixed him with a rapt gaze and an RC with ice, Camden started to describe the weary years of his brother's illness—how well at times it disguised itself as improvement!—and the cruel greeting cards from well-wishers, the false heartiness, the diabolical telephone calls full of best of lucks, which initially led his family to hope for improvement, until it became terribly obvious what would happen.

The journalist took his leave.

Camden immediately felt unburdened, elated.

That night they played their first under-eighteen club. An innocent, freckle-faced girl bought a great number of Camper shirts and told Camden how bummed her boyfriend was because he couldn't make the show, he had to work. She stood off to the side with her camera awaiting David Lowery, saying how she felt like she was in line to have her picture taken with Goofy at Disneyworld, and she requested two pictures, one with flash and one without, and then even asked David Lowery for his autograph. Pete befriended her, eventually even lured the freckle-faced girl back to the hotel. He was apparently successful. She'd never had a name so she was down in the tonnage tallies as "Freckles." Camden wondered about these special friends getting home, where parents waited. How would they explain what took them so long, why the concert ran so late? What if they let slip something about having seen the band's hotel?

The gig eroded Camden's elation. His drums still sucked bong water, and he knew it. After the show, right after the photographs and autographs and T-shirt sales, when the band went offstage, they were sitting around. For a moment it was all kind of okay, although in fact he was no longer elated but grievously depressed, but still it was okay.

And then David lit a cigarette. "Camden, man . . ."

Camden was like, Oh, about time. Lowery'd been especially polite of late because he apparently believed it would motivate Camden.

"You're not cutting IT, man. Camden! You got ten days to do IT. I can't tell you what you're doing wrong but you're just not doing IT right, whatever IT is, you have to think about IT, figure IT out. You know, I'm not gonna good-vibe you about this. I'm gonna get in your ass if I have to. But that's IT. Ten days. *What are you thinking?*"

So everyone was getting down on him, perfectly reasonably, he'd sucked so bad. He didn't really mind that they were getting down on him, but what could he say? He didn't like being mediocre at this, but sometimes he had IT, or thought he had IT, or had found IT, and the next time IT was gone, or some nights the audience would be totally into IT and he could feed off that and get excited, but other nights he could not locate IT anywhere.

They took the highway as far east as it could go and headed north.

They played Athens GA, Atlanta GA, Columbia SC, Charlotte NC, Chapel Hill NC, Virginia Beach VA, Blacksburg VA.

In this manner, a week passed.

By then the air war had been so long blasting away, with the USS *Missouri* lobbing car-size shells over the horizon hourly into remote strongholds and some given number of unprecedented sorties, with AWACs scrambling Iraqi radar and routine military briefings about the bomb damage assessments performed via satellite, and every day the stock market climbing from the news, all this had been their backdrop for so long now that everyone gradually figured there was no other kind of war anymore but this distantly targeted, faceless sort. Iraq too forgot. Its boldest new weapon was the redirecting of several million barrels of Kuwaiti crude directly into the gulf, an impersonal, roundabout sort of hurt, arguably done to hinder an amphibious landing. These sorts of unmanned tactics had formed the band's expectations for so long that when, at 11:30 one night, Richard Cheney came on the minivan's radio to say he was instituting a press blackout because the long-awaited ground war was starting and that Americans would now receive little information about what was occurring, it was actually real to the band for nearly the first time. In their name youngsters were pulling on fatigues and shooting guns at other youngsters to defend these selfish rock star lives of theirs and the band's right to gorge itself on anything and everything, fighting on behalf of this landscape of coveted celebrities and ideas like national interests, businessman-based wars, the Indy 500, the Nike Lifestyle®—cherished ideas that no one in the band cherished, much less believed, and very much did not want some teenager in a far-off country to die over.

Camden had the wheel at the time. They were driving past an apple orchard, near Rev. Tucker's Place. The moon was low in the pines. A glow-in-the-dark sign advertised homemade lemonade, available at the next right. There was an almost ghostly warmth in the minivan. "We must assume the Iraqis are confused," Cheney spoke gravely, "and it is essential we do nothing to clarify the picture for them."

A local franchise of Big Chick Fried Chicken flew past.

For once, the band had run out of jokes. At times this traveling and trawling for fortune and fame linked up in Camden's mind with what had been occurring since forever—a group of men heading off together to circumscribe a territory, to plant a flag, to sail the seas, to retake the ancestral lands, to overthrow the monarch—while at other times it felt like a three-ring caravan of clowns with squeezable wheezes and inflatable shoes crammed in a joke jalopy and sent sailing through a cloud of sawdust and cannon smoke to the smell of cotton candy. What were they doing out here, heading somewhere at midnight? What was so important? Who were they? Were they traveling entertainers? Was this a freak show? Was it really worth dying for?

Camden didn't especially like to drive. He only did so when David insisted, always after unnecessarily pointing out how everyone else had taken a turn. Maybe it was bad luck, but it seemed to Camden that he regularly got stuck with the longest legs, the four hundred miles into Tucson, the eight hours through Florida's swamps (where signs read NO FISHING OFF ROADWAY), and now a night ride out of Blacksburg through the heart of Virginia. Great stretches were unimaginable black, punctuated by the infrequent dot of a cold and distant houselight. The many cars became many trucks, long lines of axles that clogged the slow lane. The lights of distant places flickered and bobbed like embers in the tide. The strip malls were reduced to a mirage of fluorescence. The highway never ran out, the overpasses and exits never stopped, nor did the twiggy woods, nor the shining traffic cones with reflector assemblages; the brick abutments, the smoke pouring from foundries, refineries; the long embankments of concrete; the enormous service stations lit like movie sets.

The whole time Camden drove he was being watched. When he sneaked a glance in the rearview mirror to catch a sense of what was driving behind him, there was David, very much wide awake. Frequently he just watched, his eyes fixed on Camden's. Sometimes he barked too, giving directions on veers and turnoffs, warning about speed traps, and in general communicating like Mr. Schuck. It made Camden uneasy.

Camden hadn't been himself for quite some time.

Back when the total bombing missions was just nine thousand, it had been a sneeze, possibly an allergy. As the weeks passed, and Iraq's front lines set the oil fields on fire, it settled into his chest, a full-fledged cough. He purchased NyQuil the same day Radio Baghdad began broadcasting threatening nonsense phrases, perhaps coded messages or merely psychological warfare ploys, no one knew. And now, as the world anticipated the mother of all battles, the anthrax spores roiling from Iraqi canisters to spread through the holy city, what Camden had was the shivers, the nightly jitters, a fever. His head throbbed like the city center at night. He should probably stop smoking cigarettes, most likely that'd help, but he feared that doing so would sever his one remaining connection with these guys.

This was the hardest job he'd ever had. His arms bore odd bruises, were always stiff. His leg hurt. Every night he'd sweat like a hunted pig. He had enormous bloody scratches on his toes, burst blood blisters, irritated calluses, an allergic rash. To God he'd plead, as he examined his feet each morning in horror—where is your compassion?

Perhaps he was just hearing this music in a different way than the others. Like, whenever he felt comfortable and thought it was sounding sweet, Pete came back midset and reamed him out for dragging the beat. Indeed when he heard tapes of the shows taken off the soundboard, it was true, Pete was right. So what he'd have to do was push it all the time, every beat, all the time, pushing, raising the pace. When it felt uncomfortable, falling over the edge, that's apparently when it worked. When it sounded like shit, they'd tell him it was a good show; and the next morning, his head would throb like a cathedral crammed with crickets.

CAMDEN got them to Baltimore by 4:00 A.M., with unidentified senior military officials on the radio acknowledging "dramatic success." Tanks and plows were already thirty-five miles into Kuwait. Whole Iraqi battalions were surrendering. "It was easy at first," said one spokesperson. They were being slowed by the number of people giving up. A clandestine radio station took to the airwaves calling for Saddam's overthrow.

IT had been some amount of time since the journalist from the local weekly had interviewed Camden; they had all but forgotten. They were surprised to find, checking into their Baltimore hotel in the early morning, a fax of the article waiting for them. David Lowery read the whole thing through several times, passed it to Johnny, then Pete. Eventually Camden got his turn. It was

5:00 A.M. He fought to stay awake as he read it, propped up in bed. He saw that he was quoted in the article saying he was not badly bothered by David Lowery because he, Camden, was into the benevolent dictator school of running a band, and so none of this bothered him. But this was the only quote of any kind from Camden, his big moment, the one mention, the rest of his sentimental blather might as well have not even been shared, it had gotten tossed into a wastepaper basket somewhere, all the details, surrendered in good faith, about the night when his father packed several suitcases and disappeared into the dark, drunk and shouting to know what was the goddamn point of anything anymore, and how that left just the two of them, he and his mother, throughout his high school years. Had the journalist transcribed any of it? Doubtful. More likely he brought it out for a group of friends who jeered openly, rolled eyes at the drummer's earnestness, interrupted with raspberries and expressions of mock sympathy.

The article ended up being about whether or not David Lowery was a tyrant. It was a chance to pry into Camper's breakup. It quoted one of Lowery's ex-bandmates. "We were a group of people who, for whatever reason, be it job security, be it personal insecurity, did not speak up a lot of the time; because it was easier and because it had worked so far; and I think we all knew in the back of our minds that one day the situation would become intolerable." In March 1990 they were in northern Europe, up against the Arctic Circle, having toured for almost ten months and played nearly everywhere else. For too long, Lowery had been hurling things, indulging tantrums, abusing old friends. Confronted by a band that now deemed him impossible to be around,

Lowery grew defensive. "Yes, I am the dictator," he shouted. "I am the tyrant. *I'm the bandleader, man!!* If our records had your songs on them we'd still be working at Caffe Pergolesi in Santa Cruz, playing shows on the weekends." Lowery insisted that they finish the tour. The others voted instead to finish the band— immediately. They could take absolutely no more of him.

In bed at the hotel, struck by how correct this sounded, Camden let his head fall heavily to the pillow. *Yes, of course.* Particularly the words of the ex-bandmates felt right. In truth now that Camden took it all in, he saw that, ever since arriving in Los Angeles, Lowery had changed. Now he was always Mr. Show Business. Lowery could never relax, he was alternately distracted, loaded-up, short-tempered, gruff. Like something was eating at him. *"I'm the bandleader, man!!"* He no longer really conversed.

Despite his disappointment with the article Camden's eyes drifted shut. He even smiled slightly. He felt as if he'd answered a question that'd loomed over them for forever—*so that's what was happening.* Plainly David Lowery had begun to intimidate him. And that was bad, at least if you believed what he said about himself, because David Lowery hated more than anything to be around people who were intimidated by David Lowery. When was it, some recent gig sometime, that Lowery came upstage during the middle of "Bad Vibes Everybody" to scream at him, "If you slow this down I'll fucking kill you!" Well, he was apparently going to have to not let David Lowery intimidate him. That would have provided an excellent opportunity, for example, for Camden to've shouted back: "Then who, good sir, would drum?"

Camden slept heavily, and no specific dreams occurred to him upon awaking. Yellow light seeped through the curtains. He had missed most the morning. Camden rose, showered, shaved.

A fleet of squat Ukrainian women dressed in blue sacks angrily ran vacuums down the hotel hallway. They looked like Momma in Mel Lazarus's strip. Periodically their cords got tangled, got caught on ground fixtures or loose running boards, and they'd snap the cords fiercely, rippling the length of the cord. Camden, heading to the elevator, had to stand aside whenever they came toward him with the vacuums. At last one looked up, her glance shattered, bewildered, to murmur, "Bless you." He got on the elevator, exited at the lobby level, went to join the brunch.

The problem, as Camden saw it this morning (not that anyone had asked), was mainly in the touring part of a tour. He had no difficulty at all with the idea of seeing a new place now and again, sometimes making a new acquaintance, but done at this pace nothing could be retained, nothing actually registered, and he felt nothing so much as an overwhelming impulse to hurl himself to the ground like a stubborn child and refuse to get up. This journey had blown open his head. It was going down as a smudge. None of it was sinking in—that was yet a third way of putting it. He was constantly being shuttled here and there for appointments, feeling shaky at each, the introductions were frequent and difficult to follow, the people were hard to get to know. This morning, for example, at a long table in a fashionable Baltimore eatery, awaiting David and his band, there sat the music industry ordering brunch. They stirred Equal into their iced teas and slipped heavy forks through their overpriced eggs and salmon while cruelly gossiping about all the music-makers Camden liked, attributing their recent breakthrough to the endorsement of an industry trade periodical or a new hair color or a well-publicized squabble involving a young soap opera star in the middle of a Miami intersection. Pulling fish bones from their mouths, they dissected everything in this music-maker's life, cynically explaining why he got sudden exposure, taking into account everything, that is, but the sound of his music, which apparently none of the brunchers knew too well, and was the only part of his life about which Camden cared to hear.

Why did these sorts—people who earn salaries securing airplay, arranging radio promotions, coordinating a label's TV, radio, and print advertising, handling joint ventures and soundtracks—need to enter rock and roll?

Johnny sprawled on the table in perfect imitation of Pete, who sat across from him, limp and sleepy. Johnny, and David, too, were now dutifully aping everything of Pete's, his weary disdain, his withering put-downs, even his stench and sloppiness, such that the three bandmates had grown increasingly indistinguishable.

"Have you guys stopped to buy fireworks yet?" asked the V.P. in charge of cable promotions.

"No," went Hickman. "But David kept wanting to."

"I bet. That's the thing I remember most about touring with Camper is the battlefield scenarios they'd enact with fireworks. Very complicated. There'd be these big bottle rocket wars, like this one in the snow at Bard College when security came to arrest them or another time—"

The cable promotions guy halted because Pete, leaning over the table, was urgently whispering to Johnny, who whispered something back. Both cackled. Pete pointed lewdly across the room. Everybody at the table turned to see, but nothing seemed out of the ordinary.

"Anyways," the cable promotions guy struggled to recall where he'd left off. "This other time with fireworks was backstage at St. Louis at the Keel, during R.E.M.'s performance. But the band was so fucking loud nobody noticed. And even when Camper was on the road touring in a couple cars, if you were in the front car, you'd light a flash bomb, wait till the fuse got just right and leave it in the road—"

Pete again interrupted, whispering behind his hand at Johnny. The cable promotions guy gamely concluded, "And, of course, if you're in the car behind, you'd always kinda wonder . . ." The guy dropped a shoulder, angled his chin, shifting his weight to make it appear as if all along he'd been addressing someone else at the table. "You'd wonder, 'Now what did they leave on the road there just now? What exactly was that?'"

The various executives and agents, the insiders within earshot, smiled wanly at the cable promotions guy.

"I," Hickman yawned, "think I'd rather get laid."

"You," one of the A&R lackeys announced with a shake of the head. "You guys're like four erect penises walking around. I mean, that's not at all like Camper. Sex was not a big part of it."

"Mmmm-hmmm," answered Hickman distractedly. Nobody bothered to explain the tonnage game that had them in its thrall.

It seemed to the industry people that the band members were adrift, having lost their ability to connect with normal people. The musicians turned to one another frequently with excitement, to share ideas for arrangements, to make in-jokes about the Muzak resembling some Black Sabbath riff, to say something crucial about that person from that last town blah blah blah &tc. Other people's polite small talk fell like nonsense about their ears. Pete tossed a napkin scrawled with low-brow jokes to Johnny. Privately they shared a snicker. The industry people sat with folded arms, experiencing a strange cycle of feelings; every time they grew offended by Johnny's poor manners or Pete's laggardly posture, it notched up their pride. Each uninhibited sneer, each burp and fart carried with it a delirious fragrance: These guys were the Real Thing. The Real Thing was supposed to be offensive, it was the pterodactyl at the tea party, everybody knew that authentic musical genius could abide none of their establishment ways. These rockers couldn't help but be zealously self-absorbed and irreverently cursing because they were so fucking, if you'll pardon the language, genuine.

Some lady at the table was attempting to express to David that they needed to hear the CD before they could confidently come up with a promotional plan. "It's like this, David," the lady said. "Before we sell the soft drink, we need, you know, some soda in the can." David angrily surveyed the nodding industry people. He weighed one sarcastic retort after another, bit his tongue. Finally he, too, nodded.

"When I hear your music," sputtered a bald publicist with a cigar, "it's like that age-old debate of which is better, mustard or peanut butter. A lot can be said for mustard, in my opinion. And, of course, a lot has. Its late-night importance, yadda yadda, the pure tart delight and so on. Its color the very definition of yellow. But yet peanut butter, fuck knows why, stands not without its defenders. Fuckin' burns me up! Some names which would surprise a budding superstar such as yourself—important people! But whether you prefer one or the other—and there's even some freaked fuck-ups who'll like both the same—"

"While some people show no preference," murmured his assistant. "None."

"Yes." The publicist made an expression of distaste. "There's those, too. God save us. You see what I'm saying? You're nodding. You're smiling. You get me. Of course you do. Mustard is mustard and *peanut butter* is, well . . ."

"Peanut butter."

"Yes! You got me. You've been around this business, you know what I'm saying. It's not ketchup. It's not mustard. God knows, it sure ain't wasabi! It's peanut butter. Peanut butter is peanut butter! By the way," the bald publicist slurped some ice from his water glass and crunched vigorously, "your demo sounds great, Dave, just great, what I've heard of it."

The V.P. in charge of cable promotions had seen their show in Los Angeles but was too scared to offer an opinion. Nonetheless, encouraged by the others, he, ultimately, relented. "Your music showed," he wrung his hands, "a keen . . . sort of discernment. You know?"

Johnny raised his eyebrows, squinted. "Huh?"

"Like, I don't know." The cable promotions guy blanched, wished he could disappear. "A certain . . ." His voice dropped to a whisper. "Perspicacity."

Pete guffawed. "A certain perspi—who?"

"Perspicacity." The cable promotions guy wiped his forehead with a damp napkin, looked ready to vomit.

"Is that," Pete asked intently, "David Cassidy's brother?"

Johnny shook his head. "That's Shaun Cassidy."

Pete was bewildered. "So who's Perspee Cassidy?"

Johnny shrugged.

The industry roared with laughter. The cable promotions guy raced to the men's room.

Down at his end of the table Camden realized something: It's about whether the band is cute enough, young enough, theatrical enough, willing to tour to the brink of exhaustion and not play games by varying too many set lists or song arrangements. It's about catering to the anxieties and whims of a few lonely but powerful marketing people who are desperate not to embarrass themselves before bosses and cohorts. "So," a nearby executive beamed at him, "you're into the benevolent dictator school of running a band. What exactly does that mean, if you don't mind me asking?" As if in midthought Camden held up his index finger, backed up his chair, and quietly left the table. He headed into a beautiful day, determined to walk away from it all.

CAMDEN felt like a truly stupid doll, something painted and stuffed with sawdust then cast adrift in circumstances rife with extraordinary cunning. How did he arrive in this? It was as if he walked through a door into an arena of ingenious thugs. A lot of zeros were adding up in his head and heart while he just wanted to be back in Richmond, to be left as before, dully aching and dreaming.

It started out as an affront. David had said he wanted danger. Not enough people were taking rock and roll to its maximum rudeness, or some such thing. But the situation was clearly worse than that, more dire. In truth no one had seen rock and roll in a very long time. Most likely it had fled, gone where principled things go when adherents cease taking chances and bankers move in and merchants begin holding conventions. What they called rock and roll nowadays was money exchanged to partake of another pretty face and a few sound-byte lyrics. The hopefulness of rock and roll was missing—everything of rock and roll was missing—but, most especially the hopefulness. It'd reverted into mere entertainment, escapism, caricature, stereotype, the saddest sort of travesty, flash and noise and nothing nourishing, no substance.

Camden walked without watching and so, for no apparent reason, set off along the highway. Birds chattered their color commentary, flying or perched, a variety of peeps and chirps. Squirrels made their sporadic way along dew-coated telephone lines. It hurt to walk. He stopped to rest at a metal bench that'd been bolted near a pay phone.

Once there he spent a deal of time debating whether to call his mother, even going so far as to get up a few times and stand at the pay phone before sitting again. He had enough change in his pockets, that wasn't so much the problem, but what was he gonna say, he was gonna tell her hi, you won't believe this but I'm in, in, um(?) Maryland (—you remembered!) and, okay, brace yourself, I am not really happy, I'm here with some guys who aren't really real friendly, oh and you should know that yes, I do feel every bit like, like dying, and then being dead, and so it'd help if you drove over and picked me up, thanks Mom, gosh you're swell. It seemed important that if such a call were placed it be well-conceived and performed calmly, which was a difficult task, given the day's crisp sheen, the way his mind kept jumping around, the smell of car exhaust.

At the other end of the bolted bench sat a man, a woman, and their two kids. They had brown teeth, ripped pants, no socks. The man, exceptionally obese, hugged a trash bag full of clothes. When he turned, Camden saw the words on the back of the man's shirt. "If you weren't at Khe Sang," it said, "then fuck off."

A newspaper had been left on the bench. The headlines reported widespread bafflement. The Pentagon confirmed that a line of 100,000 Allied troops was almost to the Euphrates Valley, pretty much had encircled the Iraqi troops, while Radio Baghdad declared Iraqi troops would retreat from Kuwait by tonight. Which direction was retreat, everyone was asking, when you're surrounded?

Operating on some deep instinct, the obese man on the bench began to give, in an escalating holler, the woman crap for not disciplining her kids, their kids, who were bitterly fighting over the right to sit atop the family's one suitcase. The kids took to hitting each other with miniature toys. Their father ridiculed them. "Oh, now like that one's gonna hurt her, that's like a, that's like a, like a Saddam weapon or something. Like it's gonna do something!"

Camden set off again, lured past town houses that so resembled those on his own block that he was momentarily lulled into believing his apartment was nearby, and that if he just continued down this street far enough he'd arrive home. Cars were infrequent. Somewhere far off, the sounds of a chainsaw and a leaf blower, a barking dog. He couldn't get over this idea that all this time—all this time!—the war had never been real to them as anything more than a faked radio drama, and yet all along the war was real, you see, while in actuality, as it turned out, it had been rock and roll, and the band's efforts along those lines, which'd resulted in nothing, and lacked resonance, and essentially weren't real.

The sun hung back behind the 7-Eleven, where no amount of pleading could touch it.

A gust of wind blew Camden's hair across his head. Textbooks, heaped below a magnolia tree, had their covers flung open then slammed shut and flung open again by the periodic breezes. Papers came loose, caught an updraft. Most landed upon the roof of the 7-Eleven. A few were borne out of sight. One danced down the sidewalk to latch on to Camden's ankle.

It was a child's class assignment from an elementary school.

It said:

P.S.3 1/22/91

SuDam Husain is so stupid tha I

will shoot him and him Kiss my butt.

by Lewis Toff

age 12

IT gradually became tough for Camden to see thoughts through to their conclusion. It was like a seizure of some sort; it had him feeling like an idiot. Perhaps it was then—although it may've been later, at dusk, after he'd awoken from his nap, in a panic of sadness, in the hotel—that he thought of calling his room-mate. That was the natural thing to do, he realized; yes, of course. You seek the confidence of a peer, a trusted friend. We are the brothers of a generation that looks out for its own. He didn't truly believe this, but it provided enough momentary cover to consider this proposition; which assumed, of course, that he even wanted to change how he was feeling and that he'd prefer to not be discovered in a hotel like this one, bleeding to death in a bathtub, having smashed a drinking glass and dragged it through an artery or hanging from the towel rack by a bedsheet.

He picked up the hotel phone—hell, even the dial tone was comforting!—and dialed home. The goddamn machine picked up. Camden was flummoxed about what kind of message to leave. It turned out dumb. "You know that thing about, they like to say Iggy Pop said, how 'It's only good if it hurts somebody'? What does that mean, does anybody know? It's Camden. Well, hey there. Camden calling. If you're there, pick up. Okay, well." He hung up. In his mind he again heard the executive ask him about the benevolent dictator school of running a band. Camden remembered the journalist urging his feelings out of hiding.

From his room, his gaze turned streetward and settled on the sadness of a city bus, an ordinary city bus with its seats empty and brilliant, a hollow, luminous glow drifting into late dusk.

Camden repeatedly tried to roll a cigarette and each time failed. It was either a very hard thing to do, okay, or he was a fucking idiot. He opened the entertainment console, depressed a button on the radio. He greatly and immediately disliked the sound of the song they were playing, moved to kill it, then froze.

It was "Teen Angst #4." They were broadcasting a Lowery inter-view. This was a song Camden played every night but this ver-sion, plucked from the Lowery/Hickman demo and gussied up by some Hollywood producer, was all wrong. The song headed obliviously in one direction, unconcerned by whether or not you were paying attention. It held all the lure and regularity of a daily beating. The drums were electronically sampled. Consequently one heard the song without feeling its impact in the chest. Cam-den had never heard a song sound so sturdy, so mechanical, so meaningless.

It was plain tonight that rock and roll could be presumed dead, perhaps having died some while ago, but no one had the nerve to admit it.

The moon was full. Camden noticed it'd gotten itself snagged in phone cabling, like a dim-witted bug in a spiderweb. Someone would need to climb up and cut loose the moon. A helicopter crossed the horizon, refracting moonlight in its windshield. If the sun comes and goes, Camden suddenly thinks: Then why cannot I? Can't I?

After all, in his possession right now he had plenty of money, certainly enough to purchase a bus ticket back to Richmond. The only thing he would require was a bus station, and no further than across the street were some low, flat buildings dwarfed by vast acreages of asphalt. It was a Greyhound terminal. Inside, empty buses were penned up behind razor wire. Steam billowed from a distant hole in the ground. The sight of such places usu-ally depressed him. But suddenly, right now, he saw that this bus terminal represented freedom. He could go across the street and get a ticket home. David and Johnny and Pete would just have to deal with it, you know. So they'd play the last few gigs drum-less. It wouldn't be a big deal.

He imagined himself inside the terminal, waiting for a bus. Around him the people might just as easily be waiting in any worn-down government institution, waiting to see their parole officer, waiting to file for unemployment, waiting for a cargo plane full of medicines to unload, waiting to renew their driver's license, waiting to be interviewed for a job with the post office. They might be patrons, for that matter, waiting in the public library he once knew so well, so long ago it now seemed. The personnel who worked behind the counter in such a place were pasty-faced and out of answers. The customers who meandered around such a place, all of them tensed around the tensabarrier in the same zigzag pattern, dipped their shoulders and rocked to and fro as they walked, arguing animatedly with people who couldn't be seen and then spinning around suddenly, faces hot with surprise, believing they'd heard their name called out.

Hardest to deal with, though, would be the rock and roll. Camden didn't know if he could bear it. Inside the bus terminal it would blare from tiny boxes, pitched at the same volume as a commercial, something to ignore, a part of that insignificant bab-ble which everywhere pursues the public, the clattering melodies and blathering voices one seeks to disregard while riding an el-evator, ambling through a shopping mall, standing on an escala-tor, strolling through a vegetable stand. Once this stuff had been rock and roll, God! When Camden paused in any public space nowadays he discovered it draped in din, the mandatory songs and ads blasting from the mandatory ceiling speaker, drowning conversations, killing reflective moments. This was an aspect of music making Camden had never contemplated. He wondered now how far he had conspired in it—well, that was difficult to say. One never really stops to consider that there were people behind all those barraging noises, people strumming guitars, fingering keyboards, hitting drums.

He didn't want to think about this. He crossed off the idea of taking the bus home without even seriously entertaining it. Besides, by doing such a thing he'd be abandoning his kit to the band; and would anything ever motivate David Lowery to return it to him?

The moonlit clouds were fleecy and colored with violence. Beside the bus terminal was an apartment building, a large concrete rectangle with smaller rectangles periodically punched out so the tenants could breathe. Leaning forward to peer up at the apartments, Camden could see only ceilings, most of them bathed in the jumpy blue of television sets. He recalled reading somewhere that TV was rendering people suspicious, pulling them deep inside their homes so that all that remained outside, if anything, were guard dogs.

There was not a soul in sight. It was so lovely outside as to break every heart but nobody was on the streets. Where was everyone? It must be true then. At long last rock and roll had passed on. People would be paused this very instant at home or have ducked into a place of worship to reckon with the loss. Like when John Lennon was shot, but worse, way worse. No doubt that's why his roommate wasn't picking up.

Camden wanted to laugh, but in attempting to do so his knees buckled and he collapsed instead. Lying now on his side, he bent his legs and clasped them to his chest. He was swept with a chill. He choked.

A gate was pushed—the sound so lonely, bringing up youthful summers wasted in shut-down ski resorts, cool breezes, hillside cabins boarded up until wintertime. Night's descent continued grimly—the netted moon cast long prison shadows—rock and roll was dead—bells clanged mournfully, winds of sorrow swept the earth.

He could even hear someone weeping, quite nearby. He held his lips together and listened. It was a wet sound, small and sobering, an infant unable to sleep or a baby in a nightmare gasping for air, courage waning, weakly offering up its tearful surrender. Gradually Camden located himself in the hotel room. The grief was inconceivable, monumental. He realized the tears he heard were his—everywhere traffic was stalled, markets were emptying, schools were let out. Young and old alike wept for the death of an old friend. The innocent freckle-faced girl was paralyzed in a parking structure with her arms wrapped about her boyfriend, both of them speechless, reeling from the announcement. The journalist who had interviewed Camden was, at this very moment, raising a farewell glass of brandy. "Rock and roll," the journalist toasted. "It served us well, but we did absolutely nothing to save its life." The brown-toothed family Camden had seen earlier today near the pay phone nodded. "Hear, hear," the man wearing the "Fuck off" T-shirt agreed morosely. The truth swelled unbearably. The woman supported her shaking kids. In the mother's embrace her kids seemed to be melting. Nothing would ever be the same. Everything, absolutely everything, was changed. Rock and roll was dead. The father, too, could not stop sobbing.

Camden still had the radio on. He heard David Lowery on it, speaking gibberish. "—You know, when people have DATs or some sort of hard disc music system backup thing or something like that . . ."

All across the country caskets were being built, tombstones erected, but the DJ, obviously cowed, made no attempt to interrupt David Lowery with the news. From somewhere, Camden imagined, maybe downstairs in the hotel lobby, Pete and Johnny were calling their children to provide desultory comfort.

He really should telephone Marty in Baton Rouge and offer condolences. Doubtless she'd become sickened by the news.

Meanwhile Lowery prattled on: "—They've been trying this thing experimentally in certain record stores in certain cities where you go in, they have CDs of all these records, and you go in and you pick what songs you want from all these CDs, then they make you the cassette and you pick it up the next day. *The next day!*"

This must be something the industry scripted for him, thinks Camden. They would want to deny reality. "But maybe . . ." the industry was murmuring. "And what if . . ." They could not help themselves. Vast profits hung in the balance. They made up explanations. Rock and roll is sleeping. Rock and roll has been kidnapped. With hired supporters visible in the background recording executives with megaphones concocted reasons for hope. Rock and roll is not dead but momentarily confused, having banged its head and been left to wander. And yet the art form's eldest statesmen, from Chuck Berry to Ringo Starr, disavowed these false attempts at faith. Dead dead dead, they declared. The industry must accept it. Dead. Let the cold misery of rock's death wash over thee.

"And you pay so much per song," on-the-air David continued (while nobody listened), "and it goes to the artist. Just let it be cheap, I say; you pay for one song not the whole fucking, oh excuse me, CD and coating and all that expensive shit, excuse me. You won't have to put out a single and do all this radio shit, excuse me. It's gonna be great! It's just gonna inundate the public with so much music and there'll be no fucking, excuse me, setup costs so that record companies will be able to do these experiments . . ."

Mourning enveloped the land but would not touch David Lowery. He would not admit the death of rock and roll. You're crazy for thinking such a thing, he'd insist. You have a bad time on your first tour and you call rock and roll dead? You're fucking crazy. You're inside your head, having some kind of tweaked-up episode in a hotel room. Rock and roll is fine, it's you that's fucked-up. Now get to the club for sound check.

And so would arrive another showtime, in another town, Camden managing to assemble enough of himself to go track down the others. Together they would all somehow get, eventually, to the right place.

*The tenth chapter, being an epilogue of
sorts, in which the backline man
emerges, a bass drum cable shorts out,
parents are visited, a small blue dot
becomes a mixed-up boy, and some
kind of new tonnage record set*

I ALWAYS COME to stories late: I always have: that's just me.
In my line of employment I am compelled to race around a lot
trying to make sense of messes that can scarcely be made sense
of, why someone let the aggrieved keyboardist near the substance
or just who it was who drank all the drummer's Perrier, where—
at the last minute—one finds, late on a Wednesday night, an
off-size wing nut in Fayetteville or a specific 13/16" dual cabling
output last manufactured in Saigon before the war. It's my job
to study problems that just erupted and need instant taking care
of, to know intuitively where we are when the bus breaks down
under heavy cloud cover in some Dakota (North? South?); we're
due at Soldier's Field in four hours, it's too dark even to locate
the road map, plus right about then someone kicks over the bong
and there's reeky water running into everything.

Where I learned to improvise my way so well out of panic, I
can't say. It's not new. For example in college (and before that,

in high school) when I was through traveling with the football team and I would be showing up (finally!) in class, after New Year's, for the first time it seemed, just when a crucial exam was occurring, I'd have to concoct answers from what little I'd noticed of the textbook's cover. This method seemed to work well enough, in so far as I never got nailed, and got enough good grades in high school to go to Duke, and got enough good grades there to graduate with colorful crap dangling off my robe. My parents were very proud of me although, because they over-estimate me, they're positive I'm squandering my skill and so enjoy teasing me that I've gone from fullback to defensive back to now being a backline man and all that awaits me is to become a backup singer—although when I put up any resistance what-soever they pipe down, after letting me know how much they love me.

What is a backline man, everybody asks, and in most regards you can just call me a soundman (or a techie) and not be off the mark. I travel with rock tours but I'm onstage only long enough to set up the proper number of mike stands, to unspool cables, hook up stage monitors, and identify the outlets for everyone. My most time-consuming task is miking drums. People find this sur-prising (it's nonintuitive) but during a gig, with amplifiers burn-ing, drums can quickly become—of all things—the quietest instrument. So I direct the drummer for what seems like for-ever—snare, snare, snare, snare, tom, tom, tom, tom, kick, kick, kick, kick—while I find levels on the board. I encourage the band to play a few test songs, sampling different volumes and vocalists, until I feel good about the space, and I know how loud and wet to make everything.

Nobody should know we're there, that's the credo of any good backline man. The only times we are to be noticed is when some children, lacking backstage badges but too inebriated to remember the rules, manage to slip past security to interrogate the band leader about his or her intentions, or maybe to make a play at getting some sex, in which case we use our heads and fathom the correct course on a strictly situation-by-situation basis. Almost always, I must say, we step in and chuck the children right out on their asses. The thing is—and the children know this—a schedule has to be kept in order to make the next city on time. Maybe rock songs can be art, but a rock tour can't. Children sometimes don't want to admit the way it works, yet the truth is our celebrities roll into town, they yell a few slogans about how repressive or racist this society is, they complain that the crowd isn't restive enough, they get everybody boiling mad at their parents, and then they send everybody on home, collect their money, and go to the next town. It's understandable, children being obstinate about not admitting this. Observed this way rock seems only irresponsible, all these discarded tirades resembling the mines we've left all over the Third World. A child hears rock songs and conceives of a revolution that will save him, it'll destroy the untouchable power centers, the giganticness of everything, and leave, I don't know, city-states. Then he grows up a little and struggles to make rent every month, and he doesn't hear music quite that way anymore, he can even listen to the same songs but now they're all telling him how hard it is to survive the circumstances, the situation, or to handle a relationship. I'm not here to choose the proper interpretation. Certainly if you take rock music too seriously it becomes a ridiculous exercise, everybody knows that. Watching some palatial yuppies in L.A. vacuum their Olympic-size swimming pool while singing along to that song Tracy Chapman had about revolution, I wondered: Is there any opposition anymore? What does talk of a revolution mean in a place like this? But then again, I've worked with Tracy and consider it an honor to've miked that incredible talent of hers, and I've seen with my own eyes, from the vantage of an elevated soundboard at a concert organized to encourage voter registration and turnout in Memphis, her music empower the disadvantaged, so I must admit that same song still means an awful lot to some other people, in very different situations. I don't know if this is worth pointing out or not, but them's my two cents.

This sort of work has the temperament of weather. Rock tours may crew up quickly, but there's no guarantees that even a guaranteed job will come to pass. I was on-deck to do sound for Jane's Addiction and the Pixies—big-deal gigs in ice hockey rinks and the like—had turned down a lot of other lucrative accounts, when instead each band broke up. Almost the same thing happened with Throwing Muses: A lineup of nice-size venues dissolved fast as fog over Malibu when the songwriters finally surrendered to the catfight of the century. What can you do? You work the phone. You find the grapevine, you put out the word, you chat up every tour agent and road manager in the Filofax. It becomes a bit like gambling: You make predictions, act on rumors.

Such was the spirit which led me to hook up with Lowery's band. They weren't yet at the level where they could afford me, but it'd soon happen. Virgin was prepared to throw money their way. I needed to hear no more than that. I'd met Lowery, once, before. A few days volunteer work now would serve me well later, ensuring me their account. I telephoned my parents to let them know I'd be near home. I do this whenever I'm passing through Maryland. They made me promise, as always, to stop by. Don't feel like you have to warn us, Dad said, but don't feel like you have to hurry off afterward, either.

I showed up in Baltimore. Lowery remembered me: a good sign. Even better, the soundman at the 1918 Club—a young man; Paul was his name—had apprenticed with a friend of mine. A tour this tight, with no room for any crew whatsoever, requires each club to supply a soundman. But no matter how many years you've been in the business, a lot of these small operators can become territorial, threatened. I had no such concerns with Paul. He was more than pleased to back off, to work the board while I called the shots.

It became immediately clear why he was so willing to relinquish responsibility. The place was nothing but brick and echo. It occupied the main floor of what once had been the factory for Mills Elevators. You insert a band into that environment and, no matter how it's mixed, it's harsh on the ears. At best, the sound might approach the precision of a small radio playing next door during a thunderstorm. Challenged with such a place, my professional answer is the three Cs—crunch, crisp, and crank every signal—and just hope that nobody in the crowd falls dead from tinnitus.

Per usual, it was the drums that provided the most resistance. I had Paul loosen the gait, give the floor a bit more top. The mix was approaching tolerable when the kick cut out, suddenly and completely. I shouted at the lighting guy. He'd been tossing his fifteen foot ladder all over the stage, changing cells. I was close to positive he'd wrecked something. He vehemently denied it. I left Paul in the booth and marched stageward.

Turned out the lighting guy was right. It wasn't him. Our problem was a short in the bass drum cable, where the microphone plugged in. We had to make it work though, because for some frustrating reason Paul was short on replacement mikes and hookups. Fortunately we had some time. I instructed the drummer—Camden, his name was—to work the kick while I tried to weight the mike and duct tape it into steadiness. I was down there for a long while, beneath the stool, Camden pounding away obediently. I tried not to crowd him, but he and I were packed in pretty tight. I mean, I was virtually wrapped around his feet. That was when I noticed he was wearing shorts. They didn't hide a great deal. It affected him, to have me so close, beneath him, on my back; there was a visible response, one could say. He looked down. We traded stares for a few moments, just taking the measure of what was occurring. So that was when I knew.

The band did okay that night. Still, how good could they sound in such a place? No one complained, let me put it that way. The bassist held the songs together with fervent bobs of his head. The guitarist stomped and stomped, his face bunched happily, wearing a hat so silly I thought at first it must be a fruit basket. They certainly sounded like a band that could go places.

People danced, yes, but most appeared to be musicians. You can tell this because a musician, when he dances, never lets his feet leave the floor. He violently nods. He strums air guitar. He plays percussion parts against his pants. He tosses his hair around. This is not to say that I paid close attention to what the crowd was doing. I was mostly caught up in meditations on the drummer and what I'd learned in my time beneath his stool. He was, in his way, quite good-looking, a youthful aspect to the brow. But his gaze, so sincere, seemed also stricken, and the droll intelligence that was cast deep in his features possessed a disconcerting quality. His face stayed with me the night.

The next morning I ran into some of the band over breakfast. We were all quartered in the same hotel. The breakfast house was located across the street, next to a bus station. I tend to eat lightly on tour, as an empty stomach helps me focus on the work, and so was having only coffee and toast ("No other music so inspires the heart," I remember Eddie Van Halen telling me once, "as the sound of coffee brewing"). David Lowery's bassist and guitarist entered. The guitarist's hair, in a word: perfect. He had been in a band before, it'd gotten notoriety in 1985, mostly because its members were physically fit and dressed in spaghetti western outfits. They made one album and then something happened and they broke up. Once, over Tom Collinses at the Dresden Room, their backline man Simon revealed to me how their lead singer had lacked stamina. Every single show the lead singer'd blow out his voice. He spent most his time lip-synching while this guitarist—hidden off to the side of the stage—did the actual singing. This is actually not uncommon in the business, having a ghost singer or even a whole ghost backup band working in the shadows. It wasn't why the guitarist's old band split up or anything, it was just a story I remembered, another secret pried loose with booze.

This bassist fellow, I found him the hardest to get to know. It seemed he rarely said what he meant. For example over breakfast

I was telling him (I can't remember how I got on it) how Negro league teams would take the names of successful white franchises—there were the Washington Black Senators, the New York Black Yankees, the Baltimore Black Sox—but the weirdest example of this was in Atlanta, where a major league affiliate called the Atlanta Crackers inspired a Negro league team called the Atlanta Black Crackers.

At this point in my admittedly drawn-out story I was interrupted with the biggest, most unsmothered yawn. This was the bassist's response. Just in case I'd missed his point he then offered an interpretation: "We," and something hardened in his stare, "are talking serious snooze here." He seemed, to say the least, to distrust kindness.

I looked elsewhere. Large-bellied men in coveralls and machinist caps entered the restaurant. They had knives sheathed at their belts. They sat down with a thud! in a booth.

"Where's Camden?" I asked.

"Still asleep," the guitarist said. "We call him 'the Sleeping Man.' It's like a TV show. 'Hello, America. . . . The Sleeping Man Awakes!' The guy can sleep fifteen hours a day, easy."

"Pathetic," went the bassist, as an insomniac might.

After the meal I accompanied them back to the hotel. They were sleeping two to a room. Lowery and the bassist were in a distant wing. The guitarist passed all of his spare time in their room. It gave Camden primary occupancy of one room. This was not unprecedented. A quarantine of this nature occurs on most tours. You often don't feel like spending any more time with someone than you absolutely have to.

Just now Lowery and the bassist were preparing their room for an invasion of women. An old friend who lived in the area would be visiting with "some sisters ready to party." It became like something out of a teen comedy, in which thrilled nerds, anticipating their first sexual experience, confront some unforeseen twist. The twist, in this case, was that today was Sunday, and the band had forgot about the blue laws in this area. There was almost no liquor to offer the girls. This is the kind of emergency I'm usually asked to deal with. For once I said nothing. Grimly, like border guards, they tore apart the minivan. They came away with five warm beers, mostly unopened. Insults flew, tempers flared. In strolled Camden, apparently having just awoken.

"Here." The bassist shoved the ice bucket into his arms. "For fuck's sake, make yourself useful."

The females descended upon us, a nuisance of personalities and mannerisms that immediately sorted themselves into rival camps. There were the dainty babes with hair of spun gold, three of them, delicate and slender, all about age nineteen, whom I nicknamed "the fairy princesses," and there were the portly, wall-eyed matrons, probably hirsute, deaf in one ear, moving with the grace of tractors, whom I nicknamed "the evil stepsisters."

The drapes were pulled back. A light drizzle was coming down. The sky was the color of an old nickel. The beers were chilling in the bathroom sink. The bassist stomped about reminding us, in urgent whispers, "They're for the girls!"

Inexplicably the fairy princesses were left to themselves. They sat Indian style in an unlit area of hallway, between the walk-in closet and the bathroom, and busily debated the usual college English questions—like who made the better postman, Vonnegut versus Bukowski—while quoting from things I could not identify.

Two evil stepsisters sat on the edge of a bed. Lowery regaled them with the drama of watching Black Sabbath in San Bernardino when he was a boy. It had been his first concert, an eye-opening experience. The crowd had gone absolutely nuts. His tone leveled off. Abruptly he was singing to them, imitating Ozzy. The homely women giggled. They clapped and shook about fleshily. On the room's other side the bassist and guitarist stood dwarfed in a forest of evil stepsisters. Their hands moved in coordinated blurs. They appeared to be performing magic tricks.

I gave up wanting to understand. Camden was in a chair. I joined him. We watched television. Victory had been assured, General Schwarzkopf was saying, once we took out Saddam's eyes. "'Inflated figures,'" I called out, "'extremely light casualties'—what, the bodies keep floating away?"

Camden, bless his soul, snickered. The girls all looked as if I'd said something vaguely insulting. The rest of the band pretended not to've heard me.

There were better ways to waste our time.

"Here," I said to Camden. "Come on."

He grabbed a windbreaker, followed me outside. We crossed the damp parking lot. "If you want," I pointed west, "my parents live a couple hours away. Tonight is an off night for you guys, is that right?"

"Yeah."

"And then tomorrow you're due at Crawford's Den."

"I guess. Alexandria."

"Crawford's Den in Alexandria, right. Your last gig. The end of the tour. So hey, come visit my parents with me. We could stay the night; if you want. Or not. It's somewhere between here and Alexandria. I'll get us to the gig tomorrow."

He barely gave it a thought. "You sure it's all right?"

"My parents? Everybody's welcome."

"I was thinking of Pete. And Johnny."

"Do you really think they care?"

He shook his head.

I unlocked my rental car. "I'll go speak to them, tell them the plan. Cool?"

Camden nodded, climbed into the passenger seat. I dashed up to the room.

A short time later we were off.

IT'S one of my favorite drives, Baltimore to Germantown. It calls up a great deal. I tried explaining this to Camden. I always experience the landscape as from a school bus some twelve years earlier, a half-open window pouring in hickory scents, when our team traveled to face the Pelicans for the regionals. From the snowy hills and iced-in gulches the oaks and elms swayed as we passed, branches naked in the breeze, waving in support and tribute. On that day, heading to confront the Pelicans, our team solemnly pledged against everything we passed—these closed-up farm stands and small-town pharmacies, the ponds and quarries and as-yet-uncleared spaces, the goddamned beauty, as our quarterback phrased it, nearly sobbing, of this whole fucking country—that we would return as state champs. Something I like about myself is how clearly that drive comes back to me, the

cops everywhere snapping on their sirens and honking encouragement, each moment memorialized with the anticipation of our
pending triumph, and how scarcely I recollect the drive home. I
know for a fact that this is not the case for most of my team-
mates. They dwell on the stiffening of their limbs and the black
look of the hills as we returned that night—or worse, they dream
recurringly of the game's last play, bellowing at the ref and standing there stunned, rather than bothering to tackle the Pelican
tight end as he tiptoed his tentative way toward a tie-breaking
touchdown.

IF he was listening to my narration, Camden gave no indication.
Over and over he said nothing, nothing at all. I wonder what he
was to me at the time other than a cute boy, an unhappy boy,
grunting on occasion out the passenger window. I don't want my
later impressions to color this. I'm avoiding the temptation to say,
outright, how obvious it all was, our affection, and the pattern it
would assume, the trust that blossomed. I wonder what I'd noticed about him. Had I seen anything besides the surface, his
stiffening on the stool as I lay beneath it? Did I even realize then,
or was this not to be until later, how clever he was, how tender
and wry? I suspect I read a great deal into him, the allure of his
wordless condition. Whatever it was, his face, his condition, his
grunting out the window, it was also, to some degree, me, and
what I was going through. At this point I hadn't delved into a
man in ages. The casual stuff earning no mention, of course.
None of that was even cutting it—the headaches, the prepara-
tion, all of it over too soon, and then the anxiety about conse-

quences and the pang afterward telling me I was still looking. The year has just begun and with it a resolution on my part to seek an actual relationship. I wonder—was this behind my decision to invite Camden to my parents? Was I even sure he was amenable to something? Was he even likable? I cannot be sure. I only remember thinking, I truly am a sucker for those in sorrow.

Instinctively I snapped on the radio.

"Oh, this is a good show. Is it all right if we listen to it?"

He shrugged.

"Do you know this show?" I worked to fine-tune the radio's treble. "Do you get it where you live?"

"I don't listen to radio, really."

"Huh. Well, it's a good show. You should listen to the radio. Once they had Tom Robinson on it, as their guest. This was during his attempted comeback. Do you know who that is?"

"No."

Nobody recalls Tom Robinson, the openly gay punk rocker. On the radio show I'd enjoyed hearing him describe things I remembered—how the world felt like it would end in 1977, how the winter of '79 had seemed unimaginably far into the future. Also he told about a thirteen-year-old who fell in love with a man in his twenties, a true story. The man would have nothing to do with the boy because he was so young, yet the boy was too full of adulation. He could not stop pining for the man. Ultimately, after a year and a half, the boy succeeded in persuading the man to sleep with him—for one night—and that night the boy contracted H.I.V. When Tom Robinson met him, some years later, the boy regretted nothing. 'I would do it again,' he said. 'It was worth it for that one night.' A short time later the boy died.

At that point in the interview Tom Robinson played a song he'd written for the boy.

We were on the turnpike, sometime later, three quarters of the way to my parents, when Camden finally volunteered a bit of what he was thinking.

"I want to leave."

He said it like someone trapped in wreckage. As if he were giving up on rescue.

"What are you saying?" I figured I knew roughly what he meant but I had to be sure.

He wouldn't answer.

"You don't want to do that," I spoke calmly.

"Look, you're nice and all." He halted, watched the landscape. I waited. After several minutes he whispered, "I mean that."

"Thanks."

"But you don't have the slightest idea . . ." He trailed off again. And then I think he said that for so long he had been feeling invisible to the naked eye, or maybe that merely he'd been feeling invisible; later, I think, was when he melodramatically added the "naked eye" bit. I glanced over. Slow, fat tears rolled down his cheeks. "I'm just . . . ready to leave now."

I could've clasped his hand then. Perhaps I could have kissed it. I might've offered advice, sympathy, an argument for hope, anything. There's so much still, I could've said, to life. Or I might've asked—what's so hard about giving things time? I could've bullshitted about the healing properties of time, how you let it go by and slowly things happen, things change, emotions emerge from obscurity, until lo and behold eventually you're a new person, or a different person, stronger, not aching. But I would not have sounded very convincing, I am certain.

I really had nothing to say. As we neared my parents, daylight was fleeting. I could've said, just look at that beautiful sunset. But I knew better. There's no sunset that can be seen with eyes closed.

RELUCTANTLY I introduce Camden to my mother. I am right to be concerned. Without delay, she wants to know his age, his income, his thoughts on the war. He looks terrified. I tell her she's obviously wasting her talents as a budget consultant at the Institute; many Third World countries clamor for skilled inter-rogators. As a matter of fact, I hear China's seeking a torturer with years of experience and solid references. Everybody laughs, especially Mom. She knows how badly she's behaving although it's clear she cannot resist. She has been doing this to every man I've brought home since I was in college. I'm relieved when I make eye contact with Camden and good-naturedly, even con-fidently, he returns my smile. My father comes at me with a list of names, former buddies of mine he sees more regularly than he sees me. He encourages me, while I'm home, to take the opportunity to catch up with them. He knows where each one can be found. He slips an arm around my shoulders. He's deter-mined it's a bad thing to lose touch with one's past. I'm not so sure. My younger sister Stacy enters, furious and flippant. I relax into being here.

It has always been the case that, at home, nothing is quiet

and nobody goes hungry. Anybody who feels like it is in charge. Iced martinis arrive with endless heaps of blue-corn chips and lightly limed salsa. We drink out of plastic Peanuts cups as if we were about to take our cocktails on a neighborhood stroll. "More salsa!" somebody yells. There's never enough salsa, never enough chips, never enough martinis; and then suddenly we are at the table devouring lush green salad with marinated artichoke hearts and bits of chopped apple and walnuts when two dozen fresh rolls emerge from the oven, tender and steaming.

And we bicker with mouths full. Stacy is not drinking. She would test the patience of Pat Boone. She's at that age, where she speaks only in declaratives, the more annoying the better. Though she listens to rock music incessantly, she can only rail against it. It's astonishing, the force of her convictions. You shoo at her like a persistent bug. You cover your ears and shake your head. She will not cease.

"Is she joking?" I hear myself say, voice shrill.

I am the reasonable type. I cultivate the sort of consistent taste in entertainers which I think can be conveyed best through calmly expressed opinions. I patiently lay out the pros and cons as if I were the most diplomatic of reviewers. Before I can get very far, my sister interrupts to tell me that I'm full of it. Her philosophy is: Discussion of music shouldn't be logical. The term "rock star" itself, she maintains, is an oxymoron. They're chords anyone can finger, melodies anyone can hit; her point is, no one should be too greatly lauded for playing rock. To her, all rock stars are first graders, receiving accolades for the snug knotting of their laces. My father reminds Stacy and me that, as his children, we're naturally both correct, and brilliantly so. My mother, on the other hand, dismisses us all. "Popular culture contributes nothing except new ways to hurt people's feelings," she informs us and resumes stabbing at her lettuce.

Before we can all gang up on her, my dad serves the lasagna. It's so fragrant we nearly fall off our chairs. He uses thick slices of home-grown tomatoes, which bake into a delicacy with the fresh herbs in the midsection. His lasagna is always firm, never soupy. He starts with dry spinach noodles—that's his secret. This is paradise. The latest round of martinis taste even better. I look across at Camden and his cheeks are flush.

For a while we don't say anything. We just grunt like pigs, faces in our plates. My dad is serving seconds while Stacy, underage and (as her T-shirt declares) damn proud of it, sprints into the kitchen to get herself another can of carbonated caffeine.

Unfortunately, my mother starts up, asking when I'm going to find myself a real job, one that provides health insurance and a 401K. Before I can fully answer, we are arguing about music again. My sister has all the tolerance of a Stalinist, of Berija. She loves every band nobody knows. She won't set foot in a music chain outlet. She won't open any magazine with pictures in it. As for most music-makers, they deserve Lennon's fate, if you ask her. Her one exception seems to be Nine Inch Nails. Stacy regularly warns *Maximum Rock n Roll* about future sell-outs, and they occasionally print the letter. It goes up on my parent's refrigerator. Tonight she shouts that I am a sell-out. She has suspected it for years. She's appalled. She says I'm about as brave as a hero sandwich. Gutless! She calls on the spirit of Darby Crash to witness.

"Nine Inch Nails," Stacy accuses me. "You heard Nine Inch Nails?"

"He's a nice guy."

"He's not a nice guy!" she shrieks. "You don't know anything about him."

"I do."

"You don't! A band like that and a sell-out tubby like you have nothing in common."

"I had drinks with Trent Reznor. Good manners."

"You did not!" She's livid. "He doesn't even drink!"

"They were weak, very weak drinks. I admit it. Like lemonade."

"Oh my God, you've gotten so much worse. Dad—! The prodigal son has returned—a liar! He's lying!"

Both my parents guffaw. They're enjoying themselves. On one hand, I'm concerned about Camden's silence. On the other hand, I would like to see Stacy dead. She's every bit as irate. She says I look even fatter with my new glasses. "I'm writing *Maximum Rock n Roll* about him," she yells to my father. She's going to denounce me publicly.

It's hard to tell with Stacy if she's ever serious. As the youngest, she craves drama. She loves exaggerations, always has. At ten years of age, she could be found sobbing inconsolably over the LP of *Jesus Christ Superstar*. She denies it now, of course.

"Oh, and another thing," I whisper at Stacy. I am suddenly inspired. "Trent has exquisite taste in cologne. And plays golf."

"AARGH!" She snatches a steak knife and dashes around the dinner table toward me. "Take that back!"

Watching her come at me I realize I cannot keep a straight

face. I pull her close, clasp her arms to her side, and solemnly kiss her on the top of the head. She's stunned speechless! It takes her some time to collect herself. Finally she smiles sheepishly and embraces me in turn.

"Forget about *Maximum Rock n Roll*," she yells to my father in the kitchen.

Dad comes out with enough homemade cookies to rival Mrs. Field's. We eat and drink and converse politely. My sister volunteers last night's dream. This, like our bickering, is a long-standing tradition. My dad, the psychiatrist, specializes in dream interpretation.

"I don't know if I'm ready," Camden suddenly announces. Everybody is surprised to hear him speak. People drop silverware. "It's just, I don't know if I'm ready to share my dreams." Camden takes a modest bite of a peanut butter cookie.

We look to my dad, who has laid flat his hands and is squinting suspiciously at the tablecloth. "No pressure. Guests aren't obligated to share dreams until their fifth week of residence, after they've waxed the cars—but before they sweep out the chimney." Dad looks at me. "You've talked to Camden about this, right?" He turns back to Camden. "He's explained the rules, hasn't he?"

Camden drinks thirstily at his martini.

"Well." My father clears his throat. The table grows silent. "I suspect what that means . . . is . . . ." His voice falls off. Our chairs creak as all lean forward to hear. "—It's time for dessert! You like ice cream?"

"Oh yeah," laughs Camden.

"Good man!" Dad hops up and shouts the flavors from the

depths of the freezer. My mom comes up behind my chair and grips my shoulders. She says nothing. She gives me a peck on the cheek.

I sensed that Camden and I should get away. We needed to reconnect. I volunteered us to walk the dog. My parents own a hairy red dog, the style that was all the fashion years ago, purchased primarily by upper-middle-class families as a sort of L.L. Bean accessory. Stacy named him. His name is Cartoon Dog.

We walked the night streets of my youth. Each house had a family name, a list of relatives associated with it. As we got to the first cross street, a generator somewhere kicked to life, just as it always had, and probably always would, for reasons that'd remain a mystery. A pair of car lights illuminated us: two guys bundled against the cold, breathing plumes of frosty breath, with a dog on a leash between them.

I apologized then for my mother and my sister. They're tough to take, I know. They can inflict a lot of damage without batting an eyelash, almost unaware of what they've done. There was a long period when I couldn't tolerate my mother, her rush to judgment. As a consequence I fell out of touch with the family. Now I know. They're my family, like it or not, and the sooner I make my peace with that, the better. Because I've got a lot of them in me. And besides, I'm no better in a lot of ways.

Something flutters over my face. I muffle a scream. I feel the soft press of lips. I'm shocked. I'm unable to move. Suddenly, it's over.

I shake my head to clear it. "Can we do that again?"

"Later. Yeah."

"Not later," I hiss. "Now."

I grab his shoulders and draw him into me.

A jet plane flies over, lit to resemble a flung fleck of transistor board.

"Sounds like a dragon," Camden says. "Roaring."

"All I hear is someone blowing into a microphone."

"Always," Camden points out, and I can hear him smiling, "the backline man."

"After the gig tomorrow, are you going home?"

"Yeah."

"Can I drive you there?"

"Of course."

Again we kiss.

I let him know it's still not too late. If he wants, I can drive him back to the hotel in Baltimore. He shouldn't feel like he has to spend the night at my parents, with my mother the way she is, and my sister. "I like your family," he goes, with a shake of his head. "Your mother's fine. Your dad's a gas. It's fine. I'll stay, sure."

BACK home the dishes have been washed and dried. My father is in the old recliner. My mother and sister sit side by side on the big sofa, which has always been called the "Sofa of Naugahyde," as if it were expensively French and we were distinguishing its province of origin. It's time for late-night news. Camden and I seat ourselves before the fireplace and begin to unlayer ourselves. Cartoon Dog prances off toward the kitchen. My mother calls out, reminding him not to gulp his water, he'll make himself sick. We all listen to the dog splash about as he drinks. He appears not to've heard Mom. He comes into the living room and puts his head on each lap in turn, avoiding only Stacy. His muzzle's sopping wet, he's hiccuping, then sneezing. Tell me again, I demand of my parents, why we have a dog.

Stacy is incensed by the television news. We wait and wait and wait, and this is all we get? She's disappointed in the Iraqis. After all these months, it's decided so fast, after just a hundred hours of ground offensive. A graphic gives the final statistics: 100,000 sorties, 42 Iraqi divisions destroyed, 185,000 Iraqi prisoners, at least 90,000 Iraqis dead. Stacy storms out of the room rather than permit herself to display compassion.

Meanwhile, every other country is sweeping their domestic unrest under the carpet of a liberated Kuwait. Thailand's had a coup, Ireland's had several bombings, China's imprisoned some folks, Philadelphia's burning; Ethiopia's EPRDF has captured more cities; Albanians are burning police trucks and turning over guardhouses, Bulgaria's former regime is jailed in Sofía, the campaigning in Bangladesh has collapsed into gun battles. In Amman the public is beating up TV crews.

The television goes off and we all march our separate directions.

Camden and I do our night-night rituals and then find ourselves locked into my room. It's a solemn occasion, never easy. What do we do now? It occurs to me that everything, every second of consciousness, is about this moment, and it never stops being about this moment. Our hearts are in our mouths, as they say. We stand there confronting the unavoidable sight of the one bed. It's bigger than I ever remember it being.

The squeak of the spring as I sit on my old familiar bed brings it all back.

"You know," Camden says nonchalantly, running a finger over the trophies on my shelf, "I'd never kissed a man before tonight."

As a youth, lustful fantasies flowed from this room, a wondrous wet haze, an infatuation for the droll Mister Winegardner perhaps, a fancy for a janitor or bus driver, longing and ardor misting the world from view, drifting low along my carpet till it measured the room, then gradually scaling the walls to the bottom of my drawn curtains, then to the knob of my shut bedroom door, to the bookshelves filled with sad accounts of freaks, witches, and fags, to the tops of posters depicting cinema's most charismatic male leads, hitting the crappy cottage-cheese ceiling then doubling back toward the light fixture in the center of the room. I craved, I am saying, and I sometimes even got, far more (it turns out now) than any other teenager I have since met. Was it hard to be a football player, people ask, to be in a locker room with the most fit of teenagers as, sweating heavily, they casually stripped off all their clothes and conversed. . . . My God, it was heaven! I was a virtual spy, suspected by none. Revealed to me were the secrets coveted by every frustrated high school girl as, stirring restlessly in her bed silks, she jammed a soft, white hand into her dampness and dreamed of complimenting heroic boys on their game-winning acrobatics or their moving oratories when addressing a classroom on the fated plight of Ophelia and Hamlet.

And as it turned out, all this dressing and undressing amongst one another became so second nature that many of the boys, secure with the arrangement, became playful, more curious than they would probably ever allow themselves to be, before or since. It may dishearten those who think of football teams as a bastion of homophobia, but my team, at least, was not without numerous means of satisfying itself sexually.

"Do," Camden asks. He, too, is apparently lost in thought. "Do you remember how televisions used to turn off? They didn't used to just blam, go away."

"They didn't?"

He sits on the floor, leaning against the box spring. His head lolls onto the mattress, like something severed. "No, they stayed for a while."

I'm at a good angle to rub his shoulders, so I begin to do so. We're still clothed. "Oh. Like the picture'd go real small and stay that way . . . yeah, I remember that. It's funny to think of that because, well, Lowery, a year ago, he was almost popular enough. But that's all gone. Now Lowery draws so few people . . . he's a small blue dot."

"He is?" Camden closes his eyes. "No, no—I am. I'm the small blue dot!"

"No, kiddo." He's delicious in my hands, a boy entirely of taffy. There is nothing about him I don't desire. "You're just a mixed-up boy. You're not a dot at all."

I decide to initiate things. The bedside table, I'm astonished to discover, still contains my condoms from high school.

"The body," I begin, "with its many forgotten spots . . ."

. . .

LATER I ask him if he wants the light on or off. He says, simply, "On."

BY the time we make it from bed the next morning everyone has already left the house. We strip the bed, dawdle over breakfast, and eventually make it out to the car.

I put my arms around him. "How are you?"

"Fine."

I start the car, study his face. "Good?"

"Great."

"You're okay with everything?"

"I'm . . . yeah. I'm . . ." He turns on the radio. "Let's listen to the radio."

Today's show highlights music recorded by noisy bands who inhabit the Pacific Northwest. They are unknown. This does not trouble me. Many of us have been listening to unknown bands for so long, it scarcely matters. College music, they call it.

"Oh." Camden draws himself up. "Rock and roll isn't dead after all."

"Of course it isn't, silly boy."

"The other night I was pretty convinced it was."

"Who put that idea in your head?"

His answer comes haltingly. "I can't remember anymore."

Within seven months many of these northwest bands will become unusually popular. It turns out many consumers agree with

David Lowery about music losing its danger, they just have no way of demonstrating it. You can walk into a butcher's shop and tell them exactly how to cut that side of beef for you but you can't take your CDs back to the record store and ask them please for more danger. You have to wait for the right stuff to show up and then pounce, as unexpected millions soon do. Though it'll fulfill Lowery's vision, he won't be the primary beneficiary. He'll earn but a small share of the profits. It will be mainly these northwest bands who'll supply the danger. Lowery's meticulously rehearsed band will sound suddenly out-of-date, a throwback to the fashions of more courtly times, too polished, somehow un-believable. But in the car, just then, we have no idea of the surprises ahead.

I turn down the volume. "Are you sure you're okay?"

"I think"—his voice is quite low, even diffident—"I'm happier than I've ever been in my life."

I smile at the radio.

WE make good time to Alexandria. We arrive at Crawford's Den by 2:00 P.M. The stench inside is so bad we start to laugh, Cam-den and me. Then we can't stop. Soon tears are running down our faces, we've fallen into one another's arms, cracking up like lunatics. Most likely a skunk has crawled beneath the club, def-ecated a great deal, and then died.

The rest of the band arrives. They start to tell how it fared with the evil stepsisters and fairy princesses. We wave for quiet and advise them of the situation inside. Lowery ignores our warn-ing. He bravely walks on in. His nose is so far in the air it looks as if the back of his head is weighted. A minute later he comes sprinting back out, hunched and gagging. He forces the others to go in and take a good whiff. They do. The bassist declares that what has happened is that Mother Earth has just cut the world's nastiest fart. We bottle that, he says, and we're millionaires. Every nature lover is gonna want to buy a sniff. On the other hand the guitarist advocates canceling the gig. He thinks it's a burst septic tank. The only authority figure seems to be the bartender. He doesn't want to hear about it. He's got rubber nose plugs in, the type swimmers wear, and they aren't helping a bit. He tells us it's nowhere near as bad as when some guy puked into the air conditioner this last summer. A customer at the bar stirs, insists that the only thing that helps is rum, and tons of it. Everybody's amenable to folk remedies. We shrug and all put in for a half-gallon of Bacardi. The guitarist wants to know if we're supposed to splash it on everything or just drink it. By the time the doors open at eight we're utterly wasted.

It's like a horror film in which escapees from an insane asylum disguise themselves as a musical group. Onstage the band is entangled in their cords. Lowery's going to cut himself free using the edge of his guitar pick. Camden repeatedly slaps his high-hat with a mandolin. It sounds so fantastically good they all pause to argue whether they could use that effect somewhere. The guitarist positions himself at the main microphone. As soon as I get it snapped on, he informs the club he's officially no longer married. He means that his divorce has finally come through. As of today he's a single man.

I feel like somebody should acknowledge the import of what he's saying, but I'm too busy struggling over the knobs on the soundboard. They seem unusually difficult to turn. Although I can see some fingers working away, and it occurs to me these fingers are my own, yet at the same time they seem awfully removed from me. I decide I'll let the club's soundman deal with the soundboard, and I go over to the guitarist. Indeed, something should be said, I just don't know what the right response is. I offer him my congratulations and then add, "I'm sorry."

He sits on the stage. Most of tonight's Bacardi is in him. He punches listlessly at his pedals. I try to speak sensibly. I encourage him to ball up his sorrow and stuff it into his guitar, or something like that. I've clearly had way too much to drink. I tell him to really rock tonight, man, to blast it out.

"Blast," he repeats, wrestling with the pronunciation. Apparently it's not a word he's heard before. "Blast, or . . . I don't know. Cry. One or the other."

None of the words commonly associated with singing—robust, supple, lissome, fluid, vigorous, colorful—apply tonight to David Lowery. Instead, descriptions that come to mind are connected to chewing—chomping vowels, biting off syllables, smacking lyrics like gum. And yet David Lowery makes the most of this apparent deficiency by desperately forcing every word, by strangling his range, imposing urgency. It seems like something anybody could do but nobody ever has before.

Lowery breaks five strings that night. He has the habit of breaking a string and then tossing the guitar to the side of the stage, as if he were throwing it away. I remember now hearing that Camper's roadie would often look up during a show to find a guitar flying his way. Sometimes he'd manage to catch it. Many of their tours he'd spend gluing these guitars back together, the splintered necks and heads. Lowery turns one moment and he's the spitting image of Danny Kaye—red hair, strong youthful features, but literally spitting. Pretty young blond things are eager to meet the band, standing on the stairs, breasts pressed up against the stage.

At some point they can't decide which song to play and so decide they're through. They put down their instruments and leave. While the crowd whistles and applauds, the band shuts themselves in a small room backstage and collapses, panting and sweating out the rum. It's the end of the tour and they have some things to work out. Lowery asks if I'm going to keep on with them. After you get a record out, I answer, sure, why not?

Next everyone pivots to look at Camden. Since our lovemaking he looks more substantial somehow. I doubt everyone sees it. Everybody's still drunk but it's not as if they're saying things they don't mean. The crowd continues calling for their money's worth, more songs, an encore. In here, the room goes tense. Here it is, the last night, and they apparently still haven't decided what to do, whether or not they want this drummer. It's me, oddly enough, who speaks up. As if already I somehow represent the band. "How about you? You gonna keep on with these guys?" I ask. Camden chuckles and shakes his head. The band seems glad to hear it. The atmosphere relaxes. "Will you at least keep on with this guy?"

"Which guy?" he asks.

I point at myself.

"Oh, definitely." Again he laughs. "Of course." The band beams. They are happy for us. Camden stretches for me but then dizzily lays back down.

The bassist points out that the rum really works. That drunk knew what he was saying. The smell seems barely noticeable now, as they lay here, drooped and draped over crates. They listen to the fans. They begin to rally for a return to the stage. Lowery stops. He is curious how much I weigh. When I tell him he lifts Camden's hand, declares that he's set some kind of new tonnage record.

Lowery's stage patter has disintegrated. "Thanks, you came to see us," he bellows, to the crowd of fifteen. "We appreciate it lots. You guys were, like, were worth twice the amount that you were. Wait." He seems to want to continue, thinks better of it. "No," he says into the mike, as the band starts their last song of the night. "I'll just stop."